A Decent Proposal

A Novel

Donna Deloney

Proverbial Press
Chicago, Illinois

Proverbial Press
www.proverbialpress.com

Publisher's Note: This is a work of fiction. Names, characters, places, and incidents are a product of the author's imagination. Locales and public names are sometimes used for atmospheric purposes. Any resemblance to actual people, living or dead, or to businesses, companies, events, institutions, or locales is completely coincidental.

Book Layout ©2013 BookDesignTemplates.com

Ordering Information:
Quantity sales. Special discounts are available on quantity purchases by corporations, associations, and others. For details, contact the author at the address above.

A Decent Proposal/ Donna Deloney. -- 1st ed.
ISBN 978-0-6159317-7-7

Trust in the Lord with all your heart,
and lean not on your own understanding.
In all your ways, acknowledge Him,
and He shall direct your paths.

−PROVERBS 3:5-6 (NKJV)

PROLOGUE

Hand in hand, the young couple walked quietly
along the Chicago lakefront. Though it was late
August, the sun had shifted to the west and the
temperature was dropping. A cool breeze drifted off
Lake Michigan, making the unseasonably cool 75
degree evening even chillier. There were a few joggers
on the path and a random cyclist here and there, but
for the most part, they were alone on this beautiful
summer evening. Andy savored these moments. He felt
he could be close to Vanessa, but quiet enough to hear
his Master's voice. "I love you," he said quietly. When
she didn't return the sentiment, he stopped and turned
to face her. "Did you hear what I said? I love you,
Vanessa."

She nodded. "I know. I heard you."

"Okay. Usually, when one says 'I love you,' the other person usually says, 'I love you, too,' especially when it's been said before by both parties."

She nodded again. "I am aware."

"Then what's wrong?"

"Nothing."

"Vanessa, talk to me, please. If you're not in love with me, say so."

"I do love you. I was just thinking."

"About what?"

"Us. Where we're headed."

"I thought we were headed for dinner," he said, laughing.

She punched him in the arm. "No, silly. I meant where we are headed as a couple." She started walking, tugging him along. "I know we've talked about marriage, but how are we going to do this, with you going for your MBA next year and me with a couple of years to go before I get my degree?"

Now it was his turn not to respond. She nudged him. "The idea of marriage got you in a funk all of a sudden?" she asked.

He shook his head. "No. I do want to marry you. But that's not it." He stopped walking again and turned to look at her. "You do know that I'm not going for my MBA. I told you before that I'm going for my double Master's in Theology and Christian Ministry."

"Yeah, you did mention it, but I didn't think you were serious."

"Why didn't you think I was serious? I told you I got my acceptance letter from Wheaton College. I've already arranged for housing, and I've got scholarships and a job lined up." He looked at her in disbelief. "You still don't think of my calling to ministry as something I take seriously?"

"No! I mean, yes! I mean...oh, I don't know what I mean. No, wait, yes I do. You're about to graduate with a degree in business at the top of your class. You have an offer to work at the Chicago Board of Trade and they're going to pay for your MBA. That was the plan."

"That was your plan, Vanessa. I told you I had to go another way. I have to follow where God is leading me."

"But what about us? What about our plans?"

"We haven't changed." He smiled and reached in his pocket. "I was saving this for dinner, but..." He pulled out a ring box and placed it in her hands. Before he could speak, she placed her hand over his mouth.

"Oh Andy," she said, "don't. Let's not do this right now. I think we should wait until the time is really right. Let's just enjoy the evening." She took the box and slipped it back in his pocket. "Besides, I couldn't marry a poor preacher, now could I?" She laughed. "C'mon, let's go eat. I'm starving." She wrapped her arm in his and they resumed their walk, chuckling. He never noticed the tears in her eyes.

~ ~ ~

The following afternoon, Andy finished his last class and headed towards Vanessa's apartment. He was a little concerned because she hadn't answered the phone when he called her earlier that morning. They always spoke each morning, saying a quick prayer before the day began.

He arrived at the Chatham Square building in Hyde Park. The old brick building had once been a luxurious hotel. Over the years, the new owners had rehabbed it and converted it into pricey apartments. Many of the studio apartments were rented out to students at the University of Chicago, where he and Vanessa attended. He was always a bit amazed at the amount of money the building's owners had spent on the finishes. From the marble floor to the ornate light sconces on the wall, everything about the place screamed first class. Andy often thought that the owners should have spent less on the looks of the building and more on making affordable housing for the city's lower middle class.

The guard desk in the lobby was empty. Andy signed in to the guest book, then took the elevator to the fourth floor. He headed down the hall. Vanessa's apartment was the second one on the left. The plush carpet masked the sound of his footsteps. He knocked on the door of her one-bedroom apartment. She didn't respond, so he knocked again, calling out, "Vanessa? Vanessa?"

Vanessa's neighbor across the hall opened his door. "Hey," he called, "you're Andy, right?"

"Yeah."

"Yeah, she's gone, man."

"What do you mean, gone?"

"She's outta here. Checked out. Moved. Gone."

"Since when?"

"Since the movers came this morning and packed up her stuff." He came over and handed him an envelope. "She stopped by and asked me to give this to you."

"Thanks." He waited as the man watched, expecting him to open it. When it was clear Andy wasn't going to give him the satisfaction, he went back into his apartment. Hands shaking, Andy tore open the envelope. He leaned against Vanessa's door and slowly sank to the ground as he read the note in Vanessa's near-perfect penmanship:

Andy,

I'm so sorry it has to be done this way, but I couldn't take the chance on doing this in person.

You and I aren't meant to be together. Your decision – your calling – is not something I can accept. And as much as I love you, I can't ask you to be something or someone you aren't. But that also means that I can't be someone I'm not.

Please don't try to contact me. I will be leaving the country and I don't know when I'll be back.

Please know that I really do want what's best for you, even if it means letting you go.

I love you,

Vanessa

CHAPTER ONE

Shackles

Ten years later...

Vanessa Carson sat silently in the leather wing chair of her attorney's office. She hated this office, or more precisely, she hated being in this particular office. Being here reminded her of her late parents. It had been just over a year since her father's death. At that time, she and her mother had come here for the reading of her father's will.

~ ~ ~

Matthew Carson's death from a sudden massive coronary brought Vanessa home from her travels to grieve with her mother. Vanessa never left her mother's side in those first few weeks, but soon after the reading of the will, the wanderlust bug bit again and Vanessa was itching to take off. The day before she was to leave, she had lunch with her mother at the City Park Grille, one of Maris' favorite neighborhood restaurants.

Maris was already seated when her daughter breezed through and sat down. Giving her mother a peck on the cheek, she said, "You don't look so good, Mom. Did you go see your doctor like I suggested?"

"And hello to you too, baby." The waiter came to take their orders. They were frequent patrons, so they ordered their usual. After he left Maris said, "As a matter of fact, I saw Dr. Winters yesterday."

"Oh? What did he say? You're probably just stressed from everything since Daddy's death."

"It's not that." She reached over and took her daughter's hand. "I've been having some problems for a while—— some headaches, dizziness, numbness, a lack of coordination."

"Mom! Why didn't you tell me? Did Daddy know?"

"Yes. He insisted I see Dr. Winters and we had a bunch of tests done. We didn't want to worry you until we knew for sure what we were dealing with. But I never went back to get the results because of what happened with your father. Once things settled down, Dr. Winters called and had me come in to discuss the results of the tests."

"Oh my God. Is it serious?"

"I'm afraid it is. Dr. Winters found a tumor in my brain. It looks like cancer."

"Oh no! Mom!" Vanessa tried to keep her composure, but failed. "Are they sure? Did you get a second opinion? Can it be treated?"

"I've seen the best doctors and they all agree. I'm scheduled for surgery in a couple of days. After that, we'll probably do chemo and radiation."

Vanessa smiled and nodded. "Well good. That's good——I mean, we can beat this."

"Baby, this isn't beatable. At best, we can slow the progress of the tumor, but inevitably, it's going to kill me."

Vanessa snatched her hand away. "Don't say that," she hissed. "Don't say that. You can beat this. We can beat this."

"No. You are going on your trip. Aunt Phoebe will be with me."

"Are you kidding? You're sending me away? What, you don't think I can handle this? Mom, I may be a flake about some things, but I'm not a child. I can handle this, and I'm going to stay with you until we beat this."

"It's too much to ask of you."

Vanessa slammed her hand on the table, causing the dishes to rattle. Ignoring the stares of the other patrons, Vanessa nearly screamed. "Will you stop it! God, Mom, how shallow do you think I am?"

"Lower your voice, Vanessa, please."

The young woman took a deep breath and let it out. She leaned in and spoke in a hushed tone. "I'm sorry. It's just... I know I disappoint you sometimes. Okay, most of the time. This isn't the life you wanted for me,

I know that. But there's no way I'm going on a trip while my mother is having major surgery and facing cancer. No way! I'm not that selfish, Mom. That's not who you and Daddy raised me to be." She reached over and took her mother's hand. "I just lost my father. I'm not going to lose you too. Whatever it takes, I'm going to be right here for you. We're going to get through this, Mom. Together."

Vanessa was true to her word. She made sure that her mother had everything she needed to be comfortable and recuperate. She made sure that the work of the Carson Foundation continued smoothly, attending events that her mother had scheduled when Maris was too ill to participate. Vanessa made sure her mother had the best care money could buy. In the end, it wasn't enough. The cancer came back and spread quickly. Maris——against Vanessa's objections—— made the decision to stop treatment. She wanted to die in peace at home. Vanessa spent every moment she could at her mother's side until the moment she drew her last breath.

~ ~ ~

Now, here she was again, waiting for the reading of her mother's will. In the weeks before her death, Maris had summoned the family attorney to the home to update her will. As far as Vanessa was concerned, she could have received an email. She had planned a long, private cruise around the Mediterranean so she could grieve in peace.

Sitting next to her was her great-aunt, Phoebe Carson. Phoebe was Vanessa's favorite——and only—

—aunt. Vanessa often went to the elder woman to confide her secrets. Phoebe never judged, never criticized. But she wasn't afraid to speak her mind and tell the truth as she saw it. Vanessa and Phoebe had always been close. Today, however, Phoebe kept her distance. Perhaps it was the formality of the office or the reason for their visit. In any case, Vanessa noted that the normally refined, unflappable Phoebe was clearly agitated.

She looked up as Alexander Nichols, their family attorney, entered the room. He had been a part of the Carson family legacy as long as Vanessa could remember. He took a seat behind the mahogany desk. "I apologize, ladies, for the delay. Let's get down to business, shall we?"

Vanessa nodded. "Alex, can you skip all the legalese? Just tell me what I need to know so I can get out of here."

"Vanessa," Phoebe countered, "that is rude. Alexander has a job to do and you need to show him the proper amount of respect."

Alexander held up his hand. "No, that's alright, Phoebe. I understand how difficult this has to be for both of you. And yes, we can skip the legalese. I'll get straight to the point." He pulled out his portfolio and began going over a list of typed notes. "Your mother's will is pretty much in line with the wishes of your father. There are provisions for Phoebe's share to ensure that she will be cared for the rest of her life. There are also provisions for the household staff to make sure that they remain employed and taken care

of. There are some bequeaths of personal items to
various friends and charities. The Carson Foundation
will continue in perpetuity. Your allowance will
continue and living expenses will be paid in accordance
to your father's wishes. The house and all personal
property and assets belong to you." He paused.
Clearing his throat, he shuffled the papers in front of
him. "There was, however, a codicil added to your
mother's will, at her request." He cast a furtive glance
at Phoebe, who stared straight out the window behind
the attorney's head.

"What sort of codicil?"

"Well, it seems your mother was concerned about
your, shall we say, lack of purpose in life." He cleared
his throat again. "The codicil stipulates that in order
for you to inherit the bulk of your family's estate, you
have to do two things."

"And they are?"

"First, you will have to take over the administration
of the Carson Foundation on a day-to-day basis. There
is a board in place, of which you will become chairman;
you will also serve as interim CEO and President until
such time as a suitable candidate can be found. You
should also know that there is a provision within the
bylaws which allows you to serve in both capacities
should you choose to do so."

Vanessa sighed. It was just like her mother to get
what she wanted, even in death. But at least she
believed in the foundation's goals, even if it meant
curtailing some of her traveling. "Fine. What is the
second thing?"

"You have to be married by your thirtieth birthday and remain so for at least one year. If you don't, the remaining assets, with the exception of those items specifically listed in your parents' wills, will be divided equally among several charities, including the Carson Foundation. And you will be cut off financially."

Vanessa's jaw dropped. "Are you kidding me? How... how can she do that? Is that even legal?"

"I'm afraid it is. Your mother was of sound mind when she created the codicil. She knew exactly what she was doing. And it was legally witnessed by me and your Aunt Phoebe."

Vanessa turned in her seat. "You knew about this?"

Phoebe nodded. "I did. It was your mother's idea to add the codicil. She and I both were concerned about your aimlessness. If Maris hadn't become ill, you would have been off squandering money and wasting your life."

"I helped raise money——including money for the foundation!"

"Yes, but that's not enough. Vanessa, you have so much talent, and I don't mean being seen in the social register. God has something special in store for you but you've been running away from it. Now it's time for you to stand still and figure out what it is."

"I get that. I can run the foundation and contribute. But why marriage? And why now? I'll be thirty in less than two weeks! Who am I supposed to marry in that time?"

"You're the last of the Carsons. You need to settle down, get married, and have some children who will carry on the legacy."

"I'm supposed to produce an heir to carry on the family name?" she asked, indignant.

"That's my hope. But even if you never have children, you shouldn't be alone. Your parents had a wonderful, fulfilling relationship. You deserve that. Believe me, no one should go through this world alone."

Vanessa couldn't believe what she was hearing. This was all too much. "I'm going to challenge the will. I'm taking this to court. If Daddy were here, he'd never stand for it."

"True," Alexander said, "but the terms of your mother's will supersede that of your father's. And her wishes were clear. You don't have grounds to contest the will. If you take this to probate court, it could take years, and in the meantime, all of your assets would be frozen. You wouldn't have access to any financial resources. If you lose the case——and I'm pretty sure you will——you'll have violated the terms of the codicil and you'll still be cut off. Vanessa, we're talking nearly a quarter of a billion dollars here. Do you really want to take that chance?"

"I don't believe this." Vanessa closed her eyes and shook her head. "What am I supposed to do?"

"I don't know," Alexander said. "Aren't you seeing someone?"

"It's complicated. Besides, I doubt that he'd be willing to get married in 10 days."

"If it helps, I don't think your mother was trying to hurt you," Phoebe said. "She was only looking out for your best interests."

"By subjecting me to some eighteenth century marital shackles? Great. Thanks, Mom." She looked up and rolled her eyes. "Well, since I'm about to be broke, the least I can do is to meet with the foundation's board of directors and go over everything to make sure that at least one of Mom's wishes comes true——for as long as that lasts."

"I've already contacted the board. They've set up an emergency meeting this afternoon," Alexander said.

"Great. Excuse me, please." She stood and gathered her purse. "I need to make a few phone calls. Is there somewhere I can speak privately?"

"Of course. Please use my private conference room."

When the younger woman left, Alexander came around and sat next to Phoebe. "Thank you for not ratting me out," she said. "It's the only way to make up for what I did."

"I still think this is going to backfire, Phoebe."

"Maybe. But the wheels are in motion now. I only pray that it's not too late."

~ ~ ~

Vanessa's first call was to her travel agent to cancel her plans. The next call was going to be more troublesome. "Hey, honey."

"Vanessa? Hey, baby. How did it go?"

"Not as well as I expected." She relayed to Bryce the terms of her mother's will. His reaction was expected.

"Dang, baby. Look, you know I'd love nothing more than to marry you today, but I can't. Not yet. Regine won't give me a divorce without taking me for everything I've got. I couldn't come into a marriage with you with empty pockets. You know that."

"Yeah, I know."

"So what are you going to do?"

"I'm not sure. Maybe...maybe I can pay someone to marry me."

"I don't know if I like that. You're my baby."

"I know." She smiled. "But maybe I can just pay someone to pretend. I mean, we'd get married, but it would be in name only. He could live at the house——separate rooms, of course——but we could be seen and at the end of the year, we'd go our separate ways. He'd be paid handsomely and by that time, we'd both be free to be together."

"Yeah," Bryce said, "that sounds like a plan. I can ask Regine for a separation and then a divorce at the end of the year. That would give us time to work things out reasonably, or as reasonably as she will let me. But who are you going to get to marry you?"

"I'll find somebody."

CHAPTER TWO

Something

After lunch, Vanessa and Alexander arrived at the Carson Foundation's offices on Michigan Avenue. Phoebe had elected to go home and rest. Alexander introduced Vanessa to all the board members and took her seat. The senior member of the board opened up with a brief prayer and then spoke. "First, Miss Carson, welcome. And on behalf of the entire board of directors and the staff of the Carson Foundation, we want to again express our sympathies to you on the loss of your beloved mother. Maris Carson was a wonderful woman, a true example of what it means to give from the heart. Her dedication to the work of this foundation, both with her time and her money, will never be forgotten. She will truly be missed, both professionally and personally."

"Thank you," Vanessa replied. "I appreciate all of your commitment to my mother's work. I trust that you will join me in continuing to support her vision and legacy with the foundation.

"As the new CEO, I know that there is much that you have to catch up on, and we will do our best to bring you up to speed. We only have one pressing item that needs to be addressed."

"And that is?"

"Each year, the foundation reviews applicants for funding. The deadline is quickly approaching. We have narrowed it down to three organizations from the hundreds that have applied." He pulled out three portfolios. "These are the three finalists. We need you to review their applications and information and make a recommendation to the board within the next week. We'll reconvene and take a vote."

Vanessa sighed. "I'll look these over and get back to you shortly."

~ ~ ~

Vanessa curled up on the chaise lounge in the sitting room. She nibbled on French fries as she read through all the information compiled by the board. The first applicant wanted to create an afterschool program for inner-city kids that would provide tutoring and exercise programs. The second applicant wanted funds to expand a job-training program for ex-cons. Vanessa was impressed with both their application and credentials. But it was the third applicant that caught Vanessa's eye. She smiled. *The Lord works in mysterious ways.*

~ ~ ~

Andrew Perry walked into his home and threw down his briefcase. He flopped down on the couch and groaned.

"That bad, huh?" Ella Perry asked, carrying a tray with a bowl of her homemade beef stew and a glass of milk. She set it on the cocktail table in front of her son.

"Yeah. I went round and round with the bank manager. If we don't come up with the payments from the last six months by the end of the month, he's going to put us in foreclosure. And the city inspector has given us a week to make the plumbing repairs. We're going to be shut down, Ma, and I don't know what else to do."

She sat on the couch. "If it's money you need, I can tap into my savings."

He took her hand. "No, Ma, you can't do that. You need that money to take care of you and this house. If you lose it, we'll be homeless. How would it look for the minister and administrator of a homeless shelter living on the streets with his mother?"

She laughed. "I suppose you'd be more authentic to your flock."

"I don't need to be that authentic." He sniffed. "Mmmm...my favorite."

"I just felt it was that kind of night."

He leaned over and kissed his mother on the forehead. "You're amazing, you know that?" He stood and grabbed his briefcase. "I need to get a shower and pray. Would you mind holding that for a bit?"

"Sure. The best thing about beef stew is the longer it sits, the better it gets."

Andy trudged up the stairs and headed for his room. Some thought it strange that a thirty-two year old single man still lived at home with his mother. But it was Ella's idea for him to come back after college. He had loans to pay off and he was building his ministry. Ella believed that it was better for him to save the rent money and get out of debt so he could concentrate on his calling. Andy managed to pay off his loans early and with the help of grants and a few generous patrons, he had built the Wentworth Avenue Mission in the Bronzeville area. He bought a deteriorating factory building and turned it into a shelter for homeless teens and single parents. As part of his outreach, he created a pantry and soup kitchen where people in the community could come and get a hot meal. He held church services and invited local church youth groups to come in and minister. He was able to hire an administrative assistant to help run the ministry. He helped kids with getting back in school, back home, or into a safe housing environment.

The mission depended on the support of the local churches. But with the economy spiraling downward, the financial support began drying up. Andy's assistant, Kendra Rollins, spent much of her time writing grant proposals and researching funding to keep the ministry running. Eventually, they had fallen behind in their payments and were facing the shutdown of the ministry.

Andy peeled off his clothes and climbed into the shower. As the hot water ran down his back, he leaned on the wall and let the tears flow. "Oh God," he prayed, "I have never doubted Your calling on my life. I have never questioned the direction of my life or what You have asked me to do. But I don't know what else to do. The idea of turning those kids and babies into the street is unthinkable. And Kendra has to be able to take care of herself. You've always blessed this ministry, and if this is the end, say so. But I know what Your word says. You said if I trusted in You with all my heart and leaned not on my own understanding, if in all my ways I acknowledged You, that You would direct my paths. You said that if I sought Your kingdom first, all things would be added unto me. You said that if we ask, it would be given to us, to seek and we would find, to knock and the door would be opened. You said if I brought my tithes to You, You would pour out a blessing I wouldn't have room for. You said that You can do exceedingly and abundantly above all that I could ask or think.

"Okay, Lord, I've done all those things. I've asked, I've sought, I've trusted You, I've tithed, I've fasted, and prayed. I've done everything I know how to do. Now it's Your turn. You have to provide a miracle. This isn't about me. This is about the work You've given for me to do. How can I tell those kids that You are a way-maker if You won't make a way? For so many of those kids, this is their last chance. Don't take that away from them.

"I'm begging You, Lord. Do something. Do only what You can do. And I'll forever give You the glory."

CHAPTER THREE

Savior

The next day, Andy was breaking up a fight between two of the girls when his assistant, Kendra, pulled him aside. "Hey, you have to be downtown in about an hour at Cafe Spiaggia."

"I've got intakes scheduled."

"Not anymore. You really have to be at Café Spiaggia at noon."

"Why?"

"Because you're meeting with a representative from the Carson Foundation. They want to discuss funding!"

He frowned. "When did we apply for anything from the Carson Foundation?"

"We didn't. I did. I know you weren't for it——though your rationale doesn't make sense——but we were desperate. And for once, who you know——or used to know——just might mean the difference between saving more kids from the streets and us being unemployed."

"This isn't about us."

"I know, but we still have to eat and live. And beyond that, these kids need this place. Put your ego aside, get on your jacket and tie, and get your tail downtown. And don't be late!"

"What about intakes?"

"I'll handle it. Just go!"

~ ~ ~

Andy arrived a little before noon and gave his name to the hostess. She led him up to the private dining room on the third floor. He was seated at a table by the window, providing him with a breathtaking view of the lakefront. The sun shone down on Lake Michigan, turning the blue-green water into a shimmering powder blue body of water. A part of him wished he could take the day off and take a cruise. He knew there wasn't time or money for such pursuits.

The waiter came with the menu and asked if he could take Andy's drink order and provide him with an appetizer. Andy asked for a soft drink, declining to order until his guest arrived. As he perused the menu, a part of him was thrilled to have a nice lunch out, but another part of him was annoyed. The money being spent on this lunch would probably be enough to buy office supplies or stock the pantry at the mission for a week. He took a deep breath and closed his eyes. *Forgive me, Lord, for my ingratitude. I've been asked to a lunch that I hopefully won't have to pay for. I asked You for a miracle to save the mission. Please let this be our miracle.*

"Hello, Andy."

It couldn't be. It has to be anybody else but her. He kept his eyes closed and prayed again quickly. *This cannot be happening.* He opened his eyes and looked up. The body accompanying the voice was now in front of him. It was Vanessa Carson. *His* Vanessa. Mindful of his manners, he stood. "Hello, Vanessa. It's been a long time."

She smiled. "Hi, Andy. It's good to see you again."

"You, too."

They stood there taking each other in. Vanessa hadn't changed much from her college days. Her once shoulder-length dark hair had been cut into a bouncy bob that framed her face. The amber highlights brightened her mocha-colored skin and brown eyes. She was still in great shape, but she had added a few pounds in all the right places, her curves fitting nicely in her black and silver tailored pantsuit. It was a simple cut, but no doubt created especially for her. The royal purple silk blouse underneath matched her signature purple diamond and amethyst earrings and bracelet. It was open at the collar revealing just a hint... Andy stopped. His mind was wandering into dangerous territory.

Vanessa saw that Andy still worked out. He wore a bald fade and goatee, his cocoa skin still smooth and taut. He still maintained the million-dollar smile with dimples to match. The only sign of age were the tiny lines around his eyes and the furrowed brow. The brown sports coat he had tossed on over his light blue shirt and blue and gold striped tie seem ill-fitted for his frame. She seemed to remember seeing that same jacket when they were in college. In college, he was lanky and lean. Now, Vanessa noted, he was still trim and fit, though clearly he had been working out, as there was more definition in his musculature. Despite his clear annoyance at her appearance, she saw a spark in his eyes that he was unable to hide.

Realizing that they were standing in the way of the wait staff, Vanessa took her seat. She settled in and watched as Andy took his seat. She could tell he was definitely not expecting to see her. "You're looking well, Andy."

"As are you." He took a sip of water to gather his thoughts. It had been ten years since he'd seen this woman——his ex-girlfriend, his ex-almost-fiancée. The waiter came with Andy's soda and offered to take their order. "I'll pass, thanks." His appetite gone, he waited as she ordered a house salad and a glass of white wine. "What are you doing here?"

"I came to see you."

"I came to meet with a representative of the Carson Foundation."

"I am the Carson Foundation."

"Right." He should have realized. "I read about your father's death last year and your mother's recent passing. I'm very sorry."

"Thanks. Mother's death has left me in charge of the foundation. Your organization, your ministry, was one of the three final applicants. I thought it was a sign."

"A sign?"

"Yes. I've been thinking about you and I wanted to see how you were. This just gave me an excuse."

"I see." He took a sip of his soda. "You're looking well."

"Is that the best you can do?"

"What do you expect me to say? After ten years, what did you think I'd say?"

"I don't know. I don't know what I expected."

"Let me ask you this. You say you're the Carson Foundation. Did you make the call to Kendra?"

"Is that the woman I spoke to?"

"Yes. Why didn't you tell her who you were?"

"I don't suppose it would have mattered to her. Would you have come if you'd known I would be here?"

"Probably not. But Kendra would have killed me if I didn't."

"Kendra...is that your girlfriend?" She took her hand and gently rested it upon his bare left hand.

He pulled his hand back. He felt the tension building in his neck. "Not that it's any of your business, but no, she's not my girlfriend. Kendra is my assistant director. And no, I'm not married, if you want to know. But really, that's not why you're here, is it? To find out my marital status?"

She shook her head. "No. I really am here on foundation business. But I did want to see you, to catch up."

"Really? I didn't think you cared all that much how I fared, especially the way you left." He saw her flinch at the harshness of his tone. He knew he shouldn't go there, but he'd waited ten years to finally have this conversation. "Oh wait, that's not what your note said. 'I really do want what's best for you, even if it means letting you go.' That was probably the cruelest thing you could have said to me." He leaned forward and whispered, "I thought *you* were what was best for me." He straightened up and sat back. "Though perhaps you were right. As Scripture says, it's better that I be single and focus on the ministry rather than focusing on you. So you did a very good thing. Except it wasn't what I wanted."

She hung her head down and glanced out the window. "I'm sorry I hurt you, Andy," she said, her voice barely above a whisper. "I thought I was doing the right thing."

He let out a deep breath. Seeing her again so unexpectedly had caught him off guard. He was immediately chastened. "I'm sorry, Vanessa. I didn't mean to be so cruel. You have to understand, I didn't expect to see you. You show up here out of the blue and all these feelings I thought were long gone just came flooding back. I couldn't stop myself. Please, forgive me."

She turned back to him. She bit her lip, then slowly smiled. "I should be asking your forgiveness. I should have told you face to face that I was leaving, that I couldn't marry you. I am so sorry for hurting you."

He managed a smile. "It's in the past."

"Good. To tell you the truth, I really did come here on foundation business but I wanted to clear the air first."

"Consider it cleared." What was the point of holding on to those feelings? Andy sighed and took another sip of his soda.

"Good." The waiter came with her order and his soft drink refill. When he left, Vanessa began. "Now, on to business. As I said, your ministry, the Wentworth Avenue Mission, was one of the three finalists for this year's funding. Unfortunately, we're going with another equally deserving candidate. It would be improper if in my first act as CEO I award a grant to my ex-boyfriend's ministry."

He let out a breath. *So much for the miracle.*

"However," she continued, "You still have a problem."

"No kidding."

"I think I may have a solution."

"Really?"

"Really. Here's the situation as I see it. You have a ministry that is desperately needed, hopelessly underfunded, and facing eviction. And your main sources of funding have all but dried up."

"You've done your homework."

"Yes I have. I have decided to personally fund your ministry for the next five years. I will give you the money to purchase your building, help with renovations and expansion, get you up to code, and provide you with all the resources you need to keep this going the way it should for a long time."

"Really. You're just going give me a check."

"Yes."

"Why?"

"Because I believe in this ministry. I believe in what you're doing. I want to help."

"Wow. This is out of the blue." He took another drink of soda. "What's the catch?"

"The catch?"

"The catch, the string, the chink in the armor."

She smiled coyly. "How about I'm doing it for old times' sake?"

"You swoop in after ten years of no contact and I'm supposed to believe this offer is for old times' sake?"

"How about I'm doing it from my heart."

"I'm trying to figure out if you have a heart."

"Ouch." He was closer to the truth than she liked. "That's not a nice way to talk to someone who's trying to be your savior."

"I already have a Savior, thanks. C'mon Vanessa, don't waste my time or yours. Nobody does anything——especially on the scale you're proposing——without some sort of catch. So spit it out."

She ate a forkful of salad and chewed slowly. She took a sip of wine before responding. "Okay, you're right. I do need a teeny-tiny favor from you."

"Ah, here it comes."

"You have to marry me."

He chuckled. "Yeah right. What's the catch?"

"I just told you."

His face was growing warm. "You're not serious."

"As serious as your calling to the ministry."

"You are certifiable, you know that?"

"Maybe. But even if I am, at least you get what you need. And that's as good a reason as any to go through with this."

He stood. "No! You are crazy, Vanessa. Always have been, always will be."

"Won't you at least hear me out?"

"No, I won't." He pulled out a couple of bills to cover the soft drink and tossed them on the table. "It was nice seeing you again, Vanessa. Take care." He left, shaking his head in disbelief.

"This isn't over," she mumbled.

CHAPTER FOUR

Surprise

When Andy arrived back at the mission, Kendra was waiting for him at the door. From the expression on his face, she knew the meeting hadn't gone well. "Yikes," she said, following him into his office. "I take it things didn't go so well."

"When you took the call this morning, did you know who I'd be meeting with?"

"No. The caller said that we had been considered a finalist for one of the foundation's grants and that you needed to meet with a representative for lunch. Why? Who was there?"

"Vanessa."

"Vanessa who?" Realization dawned. "Oh...oh, your Vanessa!"

"She's not my Vanessa." Not anymore.

"Ooooh, that had to be interesting. Well, how did it go? What did she say?"

"How do you think it went?"

"Okay, but what did she say?"

"She said she wanted to fund the mission for five years."

Kendra began dancing in the small office. "Hallelujah! Yes! Thank you, Lord!" She stopped and looked at her boss. "Why am I the only one doing some shouting?"

"I turned her down."

"You what!"

"I turned her down."

"Are you out of your mind? We are five minutes from being shut down and you turn down an offer to keep us open another five years? What is wrong with you?"

"I couldn't accept the terms of her offer."

"Which were?"

"She wants me to marry her."

Kendra's mouth dropped open as she sunk down in the seat across from the desk. "Wow. I've heard of rich people doing some crazy stuff, but this is too deep." She sat back, shaking her head. "Okay, here's what I think. You should marry her, get the money then get it annulled."

"You're not serious."

"I am! Look, Andy, I know you take the Bible literally."

"Don't you?"

"I do, but hear me out. I think this is a sign from the Lord."

"Really."

"Yes. We are desperate. God knows we need a miracle. And now He sends your ex-fiancée and she has money. All she wants is to reconnect with you. You told me you wanted to marry her, right?"

"Yeah, ten years ago, before she ditched me."

"So it's clear to me that you're still hung up on her."

"I am not."

"Yes you are. You didn't even want me to apply for funding from her family's foundation. If that's not hung up, I don't know what is."

"Even if that were true——and it's not——I can't commit to a marriage to her. Marriage is a holy ordinance, not to be entered into lightly, but reverently, soberly," he declared, reciting a familiar line from his ministers' handbook.

"I know all that. But what if this is God's answer? What if it's his plan to save the mission and bring the two of you together again? You should at least consider the possibility."

He glared at her. "I don't believe you're even suggesting such a thing. You know what? You should probably get back to work. I'll bet there are other funding proposals you should follow up on." He turned to his computer to check his emails. "And bring me today's intake forms, please."

She stood and mock-saluted him. "Yes sir, Mon Capitan." As she left Andy's office, a thought occurred to her. She had some phone calls to make.

~ ~ ~

Andy usually stayed into the evening at the mission, but after his unpleasant lunch encounter, he was in no mood to be around anyone, much less troubled teens. He turned the operations over to his volunteers and headed home. His head was pounding from a lack of food. He hoped to grab a bowl of leftover stew and retreat to his room to relax, meditate, and figure out his next steps.

The first thing he noticed upon entering the house was the beautiful bouquet of flowers that adorned the mahogany living room table. It was large enough to be a funeral spray. "Mom?" he called out. Had someone died?

Ella came out of the dining area grinning. "Hey, baby." She gave her son a big hug and leaned up to give him a kiss on his cheek. "I'm glad you're home early."

"Is everything okay? Did somebody die?"

She laughed. "Everything's fine. What gave you that idea?"

He gestured towards the flowers. "What's with that?"

"We have company. Come on in to the dining room." She led him down the narrow passageway.

"Don't tell me——I've got a new daddy."

She slapped him on the arm. "Don't be silly, boy."

Andy's father had passed away while he was a teenager and Ella had only recently begun "courtin'," as she called it. They entered the dining room and the first thing he noticed was the spread of food. The next thing he noticed was the company——Vanessa. He shook his head. "Unbelievable. What are you doing here?"

"Andrew! That's no way to speak to our guest," Ella admonished.

"Mom! You do know who that is, right?" he hissed.

"Of course, I remember Vanessa. She stopped by to say hello."

Vanessa waved meekly. "Hi, Andy. I'm sorry to drop by unannounced."

"You seem to be making a habit of that," he muttered, earning a pinch on his arm from his mother. "Dang, Mom!"

"I don't care who she is or what she's done, that's no cause for you to be rude, Andrew Perry."

"Yes, ma'am."

Vanessa stifled a chuckle. "Your mother insisted I stay for dinner. I didn't want to impose, so I had something brought in. I wasn't sure what you liked, so I ordered a little bit of everything. I figured you'd be hungry since you didn't eat anything at lunch."

He opened his mouth to make another crack, but the look from his mother stopped him cold. "That was very sweet of you, dear," she said. "Baby, go upstairs and get washed up and changed into something comfortable. In the meantime, Vanessa and I can finish our chat." She took a seat and motioned for Vanessa to be seated.

Andy took in a long slow breath and let it out. There was no point in arguing with Ella Perry. Her word was law. "Yes, ma'am. Excuse me, ladies." He turned and went back out the way he came and headed upstairs. *Is this some kind of cruel joke, Lord? Why her? Why now?*

Trust in Me.

Fine. Whatever. He quickly washed up and changed into jeans, a polo shirt, and dock shoes. By the time he arrived back downstairs, the women were chatting like old friends. "Sit down," his mother said, "and bless the food."

Andy did as he was instructed and they all dug in. Vanessa had ordered from a local soul food restaurant, resulting in a feast fit for the Thanksgiving table. Remembering his mother's warning to be on his best behavior, he managed to have a pleasant conversation with Vanessa, catching up on his life after graduate school and how he began the mission. Vanessa regaled them with tales from her travels, including some of the more downtrodden places she had visited in Africa and Asia. It made her realize the importance of the work of her family's foundation. She knew she had been blessed with a life of privilege; she wanted to help spread the same blessing to those who needed it most.

"That's why I'm here," Vanessa said. "I really want Wentworth Mission to succeed." She reached into her Prada tote, pulled out some papers, and pushed them toward Andy. "That's for you."

He reluctantly took them. Scanning them, he looked up in disbelief. "This is the deed to our building. And the mortgage is paid in full. When? How?"

"You never gave me a chance to talk to you during lunch. I wanted to do this for you, but I didn't want you to think it was tied to my offer. Even if you turned me down, I wanted you to have this. It's one less thing you have to worry about."

"Oh, hallelujah!" Ella exclaimed.

"I can't accept this," Andy said. He shoved the papers back at his ex.

"What? Baby, this is the answer to your prayers."

"I don't like the terms, Ma."

"There are no strings attached, Andy. The building's yours," Vanessa said.

"Still."

"Still what? Do you want me to go back to the bank and have them reinstate the mortgage that you can't afford? Should I stop payment on the check and let them foreclose on you?"

"That's not the point. You can't bribe me."

"This isn't a bribe. It's a gift." She stood. "You don't want to accept my deal, that's fine. But this can't be undone. The building is yours whether you want it or not." She turned to Ella. "Mrs. Perry, thank you for your forgiveness and your hospitality. I hope we keep in touch."

Ella held up her hand. "You're not going anywhere, Vanessa. Sit down, please."

"Mother."

She ignored him. "I want to apologize on behalf of my hard-headed and ungrateful son. I don't know what's gotten into him lately, but that's not the way I raised him. Please, take your seat." As the younger woman sat back down, Ella turned to her son, who was fuming. "You better thank this girl for what she's done——not just for you, but for all those children and babies. Speak up——now."

He scowled at his mother, earning an equally stern look from Ella. Duly chastened, he said, "I apologize, Vanessa. I do thank you for your generous contribution on behalf of the Wentworth Avenue Mission. But I'm still not taking that deal."

"Now about that deal," Ella began.

"She told you?"

"Of course she did. What do you think we talked about when you weren't here? She told me everything. And I think you should accept."

Andy was shocked. "Are you serious? Ma, you think I should enter into a marriage for money?"

"Ordinarily, I would never advocate for such a thing. But there's too much at stake for both of you to not do it. The least you can do is hear her out——especially since she brought us dinner." Ella stood and started clearing the table. "You two need to talk. Take her for a walk around the block. And listen to what she has to say."

Andy rolled his eyes. He stood and extended his hand. "Shall we?" Vanessa chuckled. No matter how grown you got, you still had to do as your mother said. She gathered her tote, but Andy said, "Leave it here. It'll be too much temptation for the hypes in the neighborhood, and I don't feel like running them down."

They left the brownstone and began walking down the block. "Tell me something. Why did you come here tonight?"

"After your rather rude departure, I got a call from your assistant, Kendra. She had spoken to your mother and it was her idea that I come over and we try to work things out."

"Remind me to thank her later," he muttered. "Well, you snowed my mother——which isn't easy, by the way——and I can't lie to her, so you might as well tell me what this is all about."

She shrugged. "It's not that complicated. According to the terms of my mother's will, I have to be married by my thirtieth birthday and stay married for at least a year in order to retain control of the foundation and gain the bulk of my family's estate. And before you ask, it's not the money——though that's part of it. The foundation was my mother's legacy and the work that they do is important. I don't want to let that fall apart, and I don't want it out of the family's hands. I figure I can do what I need to do and fulfill my mother's wishes."

"Why me? Don't you have a boyfriend or some other friend to help you out?"

"There is someone, but we can't be together now."

"Why not?"

"He's married."

"I see." He couldn't envision the Vanessa he knew getting involved with a married man. He masked his disappointment. "And there's no one else?"

"No one else I trust. I know guys I could ask, but they'd be expecting a share of my family's fortune or try to trade on our name for their own purposes, purposes that wouldn't reflect well on our family. And

there are some who would love to do it, and then expose
the marriage as a fraud just to humiliate me and my
family. I can't let that happen."

"How do you know I'm not one of those people?"

"Because you've always been a man of integrity.
That's one of the things I loved about you. The minute
I mentioned this deal, you shut me down without
hesitation. I know the only reason you're even
bothering to listen to me is because I'll go back in and
trick on you to your mother." They shared a laugh,
envisioning how that conversation would end. "I know
I'm asking a lot from you, Andy, especially after
everything that I put you through." She stopped him
and turned to face him. "I want to apologize for the
way I left things. It wasn't fair to you. But at the time, I
thought it was the right thing to do for both of us. I'm
so sorry for hurting you. Even if you can't find it in
your heart to help me out, I do hope you'll forgive me."

He wanted to be angry with her, but he couldn't.
The sincerity in her words and her eyes convinced him.
"I do forgive you, Vanessa. I did a long time ago."

She hugged him and he surprised himself by
returning the hug. They resumed their walk. He shook
his head. I can't believe I'm even entertaining this
cockamamie scheme. "Okay. I'm not saying that I'm
going to do this, but if I did, what exactly would it
entail?"

"Well, you'd have to move into my house. We'd have
separate bedrooms, of course. We'll have to attend
some social functions together and there will probably

be some publicity. I'll try to keep you out of it as much as possible."

"I'm not so worried about me," he responded, "but I don't want my kids or volunteers harassed by the press. And I don't want my mother being followed or being picked on."

"So you're saying you'll do it?"

"Not yet. I have my own conditions."

"Name them."

"First, if I live at your house, I want my share of mother's mortgage paid each month."

"I'll take care of the whole thing."

"That'll be up to her. Second, you'll have to spend some time down at the mission."

"Doing what?"

"Whatever is needed. If you're going to support a cause, you should at least know as much as you can about it. It will help with any publicity you——we—— have to do."

"I can do that."

"Third, besides the upgrades needed to pass inspection, I want enough money to give Kendra a decent raise and hire on a couple of full-time staffers——security, counselors, and tutors."

"Done."

"Last——and this is a deal-breaker——you can't be seen around town with your so-called boyfriend. He can't drop by for visits, even if I'm not home. If the press is going to be lurking around as you say, the mission can't afford the scandal. And I'd bet neither can you."

"Agreed." She extended her hand and he shook it.

"I can't believe I'm doing this. I'm getting married in less than a week."

"Less than a week?"

"You did say you have to be married before you turn 30, right? That's a week from tomorrow."

Her smile grew larger. "You remember my birthday?"

He lowered his head. "Some things are hard to forget. Each year on your birthday, I said a prayer for you that you were doing well and happy."

Her eyes filled with tears. "I can't believe you still thought of me. The way we... the way I left things... I'm surprised you didn't curse my name. I appreciate your kindness."

"I couldn't help it. As much as I hated how things ended, I never wanted anything bad to happen to you."

"You are amazing."

It was his turn to smile. "Why, yes, I am." He didn't flinch when she slapped him on his hand.

She slipped her arm around his. He didn't remove it. "Can I ask you something?"

"Shoot."

"Why are you agreeing to help me?"

He paused before he answered. "A couple of reasons. First, the mission needs help, more help than I can generate. And if you're willing to help, I'd be a fool not to do what I have to do. It's not illegal, so I have no reason not to do it."

"What about your feelings about marriage? It was clear at lunch and dinner that you thought a marriage of convenience was out of the question."

"I believe in the holiness of marriage, yes. But I'm reminded that in the Old Testament scriptures, marriages were not necessarily based on love, but based on the arrangements that benefitted both families financially. They were business transactions. Yes, they often resulted in the couple being in love, but it wasn't a requirement. So, Vanessa, I will marry you and honor my vows, just as long as you honor our agreement."

"You've got yourself a deal."

~ ~ ~

Wednesday morning, Andy went to work as usual. Kendra was making coffee in the modest pantry. "Hey," he said, "I need you to contact one of the volunteers to see if someone can handle intakes on Friday."

"Why?"

"Because we're going to a wedding."

CHAPTER FIVE

Moving

After leaving Andy and Ella on Tuesday evening, Vanessa contacted her attorney to relay the news of the deal with Andy. Alexander assured Vanessa that everything would be taken care of. He drew up a prenuptial agreement, complete with the agreed upon stipulations. Wednesday afternoon, they drove to the County Clerk's office in Bridgeview to apply for their license. On Thursday, Andy packed up his things and spent most of the day in prayer. On Friday morning, Andy and Vanessa, along with Ella, Kendra, Phoebe, and Alexander, exchanged vows in the judicial chambers of Alexander's best friend, to provide the couple with the utmost discretion. Alexander arranged to file the marriage license on Monday at the clerk's office.

For the reception, the wedding party went to lunch at Café Spiaggia. Andy noted with irony that they were being served by the same waiter who had waited on him last week when he met with Vanessa–his wife–just four days ago. If he noted the change in their relationship, he didn't say anything. But he did smile when he brought the table a bottle of champagne. It was Phoebe who proposed the toast, welcoming Andy and Ella into the family and wishing for a long and successful marriage. Everyone burst into laughter, much to Phoebe's chagrin.

The lunch done, Kendra headed back to work and Ella went home to rest. Alexander took Phoebe to an afternoon meeting she had scheduled, leaving the newlyweds a chance to get settled in. The movers had picked up Andy's things and transported them to Vanessa's house earlier that morning. Vanessa drove her husband to the house in Highland Park. Andy softly whistled when he saw the size of the grounds. "Welcome to the Lifestyles of the Rich and Famous."

"I've seen much bigger, even in this neighborhood. But I hope you'll be comfortable here. Everything you see is for your use. We have both an indoor and outdoor pool and a fitness room. I'll introduce you to the staff and then show you around."

"You have staff?"

She laughed. "Yes. They've been a part of the household for years. They're like family. They'll love you."

He shook his head. "You know, I knew your family had money. I just never realized how much."

"Clearly, you never read the society pages."

"I didn't have much time to read anything except for required reading for classes and my Bible. Between classes and my job and you, there was little time for anything else."

They parked in the driveway and a tall, gray-haired gentleman in a dark suit came around the driver's side door to open it for Vanessa. "Welcome home, Miss Carson." Then glancing at Andy exiting the vehicle, he amended, "I should say, welcome home, Mrs. Perry."

Vanessa giggled. "Jackson, I've told you many times, I prefer to be called Vanessa."

"As you wish," he replied, a faint English accent marking his words, contrasting his dark skin.

Vanessa walked around the car to stand with Andy. "Andy, this is our chauffeur, Jackson. Jackson, my husband, Andrew Perry."

"Welcome, Mr. Perry," Jackson said, bowing slightly.

"Please, call me Andy." He grimaced when his offer to shake hands was politely refused by the driver.

"Jackson follows very strict British protocols," Vanessa whispered. "Don't take offense."

"I see."

"The rest of the staff is waiting for you in the foyer," Jackson said, ignoring the side conversation. "Will you be departing the grounds this evening?"

Vanessa looked at Andy, who shook his head. "I don't think so, Jackson. We're going to stay in for the evening."

"Very good, Miss Vanessa, Mr. Andrew." He took the keys from her and drove the car into the garage.

"Are all the staff like that?"

"Well, yes and no." They started walking up the walkway towards the front door. "They're all friendly, but they don't cross the line. Jackson has been with us since I was born. He is the de facto chief of staff. Aunt Phoebe convinced him to relocate and work for us when she was on one of her trips overseas. The rest of the staff was hired by my mother, with Phoebe's approval, of course."

"Of course."

As they approached the massive cherry oak door, it opened up as if on cue. Vanessa stopped short of entering and turned to Andy. "What?"

"We're newlyweds, remember?"

"Oh, please." When she didn't move, he took the hint. Instead of scooping her up in his arms, he knelt down and flung her over his shoulder in a fireman's carry. Her squeals turned into laughter as he set her down in front of the amused staff. "Welcome home, Mrs. Perry."

"You are terrible." She shook herself to regain her composure. "Everyone, as you can guess, this is my husband, Andrew Perry. He's quite the joker."

"That I am," Andy said. "Please don't stand on ceremony around me. I'm just Andy." He turned to the youngest woman standing there. "And you are?"

"Adriana," the woman replied. "Adriana Mosquera. It's a pleasure to meet you, Mr. Perry."

"It's Andy, please."

She smiled. "Okay, Mr. Andy. I take care of the upstairs bedrooms and bathrooms. If you need anything, please don't hesitate to ask."

"Thank you, Adriana." He turned to the older woman standing beside her and extended his hand. "And you are?"

"I am Eldora Wolske, Mr. Andy, but everyone calls me Dora." The fifty-ish woman shook his hand and returned his smile. "I handle the downstairs area, except the kitchen."

"That's my domain." They turned as a dark-skinned, heavyset woman made her way down the hall towards the foyer. She wiped her hands on her apron and stood in front of the couple. She glanced up and down at Andrew, sizing him up. "Um-hmm. I'm Carrie, and I run the kitchen. You need to eat."

Shocked, Andy took a step back. "I eat."

"Not enough. But we'll get some meat on your bones soon enough." She hugged Vanessa tightly. "And we'll get you fattened up in time to start having some babies. It's too quiet around here, Miss Vanessa."

"Carrie, I told you, don't start on me about having children."

"Hmmph. I expect we'll be seeing some around here soon enough. I just wish your folks had lived to see them, God bless their souls." She turned to Andy. "Anything you want, you just ask. I can cook almost anything and if I don't know how, I'll figure it out. Miss Vanessa didn't give me much time to fix a proper wedding dinner or tell me what you like, so I hope you don't mind what I whipped up. If you've got preferences, just give me a list and when I head to the store, I'll pick it up." She turned to go. "Dinner will be ready by six. No need to dress unless you want to."

Vanessa shook her head. "Don't mind Carrie. She's been here as long as I can remember. She's like the grandmother I never had." She turned to Adriana. "Is everything ready upstairs?"

The girl nodded. "Yes, ma'am. I had all of Mr. Andy's things put away as you requested."

"Good. I'm going to show Andy around the house. Why don't you both take the rest of the afternoon off?"

"Thank you, ma'am," Dora replied. "We'll be available if you need us." The two women exited down the same hall that Carrie disappeared down.

"Well, that was fun," Andy said. "Anybody else I should meet?"

"Well, there's the gardener and the pool guy, but they only come around once a week. You'll meet them next week. Let me show you around."

The first floor consisted of a great room off the foyer. Vanessa explained it was where they entertained guests. There was a formal dining room, a sitting room and a library along with two guest bathrooms. Phoebe had a bedroom suite on the first floor that was closed off to visitors. The fitness room, near the rear of the house, contained state-of-the-art equipment, including a free-weight area. The kitchen, where Carrie was doing her cooking, was huge. Besides the massive kitchen space, there was a large counter for sitting and a smaller dining area. The rear of the kitchen had French doors, which opened to an outside deck, complete with a full service kitchen, bar, and a massive gas barbeque grill. There was also a fire pit and a well-hidden sound system made especially for outdoor parties. There was an outdoor Olympic-size swimming pool with four cabanas. An enclosed pool house also contained a smaller indoor pool, Jacuzzi, showers, and a changing area. Another two-story building attached at the rear of the house contained the staff apartments. Each of the staff had their own spacious studio. Vanessa explained that during their off hours, the staff was allowed to use the resources of the household, as long as there were no other guests around.

As they wrapped up the tour on the main floor, standing in the foyer was a young woman with a curious expression on her face. Vanessa went over and gave her a hug. "Pam, it's so good to see you."

"You too," Pam responded, puzzled. She took a step back and looked Andy up and down. "Pamela Tyler," she said, extending her hand. "I'm Vanessa's publicist and a very dear friend. And you are?"

"Andrew Perry," he replied, shaking her hand. "Everyone calls me Andy. I'm Vanessa's...well, I'm her husband."

"Husband!"

"Um, Andy, could you excuse us? Pam and I have some things to discuss," Vanessa said.

"You can say that again," Pam said, as Vanessa pulled her down the hallway.

"Guess I'll go unpack," Andy muttered.

CHAPTER SIX

Husband

"Husband!"

"Yes," Vanessa answered, closing the door to the study.

"Husband!"

"Will you stop saying that?"

"You'll forgive me if I'm still in a state of shock. He did say husband, didn't he? I didn't hear him wrong? Husband, as in man and wife 'til death do you part?"

"Yes and no."

Pam shook her head and sat down in one of the leather chairs. She brushed her long braids back behind her ears. "Back up. When did this happen?"

"This morning."

"And I wasn't invited?"

"Only because we were trying to keep it quiet."

"How do you—Vanessa Carson—manage to get married and keep it quiet?"

"By doing it in the judge's chambers. Alexander Nichols called in a favor to a friend of his. If you had been there, someone might have seen you and tried to figure out what was up." Vanessa took a seat across from her friend. "I'm sorry I didn't tell you what was going on."

"What exactly is going on? Who is this guy? Is this the mystery guy you've been seeing but won't tell me about?"

"No. I've known Andy for years. We dated back in college."

Realization dawned on Pam's face. "That's him? The guy who broke your heart?"

"To be fair, I broke his heart. I broke it off."

"Why?"

Vanessa shrugged. "He wanted to get married. My family thought it was a bad idea."

"Is he a serial killer?" Pam whispered.

"No!" Vanessa laughed. "He wanted to get into full-time ministry. My parents would have cut me off if I went through with it. I wasn't ready to live a life of poverty. So I ended it."

"Really."

"Yes, really."

"Fine. I'll accept that for now. But what's with the sudden nuptials? He just shows up out of the blue and you fall for him again?" Her eyes widened. "You're not pregnant, are you?"

"Pam!"

"I'm just asking. These things will come up once the press finds out–and they will find out. It's only a matter of time. So, do me a favor and tell me why you got married."

Vanessa quickly explained Andy's situation and the codicil to her mother's will. "So we worked out a deal. He gets what he needs and I get what I want."

Pam shook her head in dismay. "I don't believe you did this. Why didn't you talk with me first?"

"Because there wasn't time. Besides, I know what you would have said."

"I would have said you were making a huge mistake. What's to stop him from 'accidentally' leaking this to the press?"

"Andy would never do that. He's a man of principle and integrity. He's also a minister."

"He's still a man." She grinned at a thought. "What if he expects you to perform your wifely duties?"

Vanessa laughed. "That's not going to happen. He understands this is strictly business. We're sleeping in separate bedrooms."

"Uh-huh. Who else knows about this so-called marriage?"

"Besides you, Aunt Phoebe, Alexander Nichols, his mother, the judge, and Andy's assistant, Kendra Rollins. Well, the staff knows about the marriage, but not the agreement."

"What if somebody talks? Vanessa, when–not if–this comes out, do you know what it will do to your reputation? The tabloids will have a field day. And the damage to the Carson Foundation may be devastating."

"That's why I called you. I knew if anyone would know how to handle this, it would be you."

"Yeah, yeah, whatever. I need a tall, stiff drink and some Advil." She stood. "I'll talk to you later."

CHAPTER SEVEN

Welcome

Vanessa found Andy waiting at the top of the stairs. "I didn't want to invade anyone's privacy," he said, "so I waited for you to show me my room."

"Thanks, but there's nobody here but us."

"Is everything okay? Your friend seemed pretty shook up seeing me here."

"She'll be fine. We caught her off guard. It's her job to protect me from the press. I just love throwing her a curveball every now and then. If she weren't my friend, she probably would have quit."

"If I were her, I would have quit too."

"She loves me. She'll work it out. Come on, let me show you to your room."

There were four bedroom suites, each with their own bathroom. Vanessa took Andy to the master bedroom suite. "This was my parents' bedroom. This is your room, now."

Andy shook his head. "No, I couldn't stay here."

"Of course you can. After Daddy died, Mother couldn't stand being in the room, so she converted one of the guest suites into her room. Besides, Daddy's tastes were too masculine for Mom, but she didn't have the heart to change it. I think you'll be comfortable here." She opened the doors and Andy let out a soft, "Whoa."

The furniture was a deep mahogany; it was clear to Andy that it was not just a veneer. It had been polished to shine. On either side of the four-poster king sized bed was a nightstand. Adriana had taken the time to put some of Andy's family photos in place. The room was decorated in hues of brown, blue, and green, softening the interior. Hanging across from the bed was a 42-inch plasma TV. Vanessa pointed out a Bose sound system in the room. "You don't have to worry about disturbing anyone. The rooms are soundproof." Just off the bedroom was a walk-in closet. Adriana had unpacked all of his clothes and shoes and organized them according to color and type of clothing. There was also a full bathroom, complete with shower and tub.

The final touch was a sitting area that had been converted into a mini-office. "My father picked out the furniture, but I had the computer system upgraded. There's a laptop also that you can use, and we have wireless capabilities throughout the house. If there's anything you want to change, let me know."

Andy gingerly touched the smooth surface of the desk. "It's very nice. In fact, it's way too much. I can take a smaller room."

"Nonsense. Adriana already laid everything out and it would be a waste of her time to redo everything. Besides," she added with a smile, "it suits you." She turned to leave but stopped. "There's an intercom system if you need to reach the staff."

"Where's your room?"

"On the other end of the hall."

"Can I see?"

She shrugged. "If you want." He followed her down the hall, noting the two smaller bedrooms and extra bathroom along the way. At the end of the hall, she stopped at the double doors. "You know I don't let just anyone into my sanctum. But you are my husband, so I guess it's okay."

"I'm honored."

She opened the doors and stepped inside. Andy noted the scent in the air. "Lavender and jasmine."

"You remembered."

"They were your favorites."

Indeed, the entire room was accented in hues of purple and lavender. It felt comfortable without being too childish. The layout of the room was nearly identical to his except it had a more feminine feel to it. He glanced around and stopped. On top of the bookshelf was a framed picture of the two of them taken in college at the homecoming dance. Andy smiled as he picked up the frame, remembering how the picture came to be. Instead of a traditional pose, she had leaned into him and glanced back and up at his face. He had leaned in to kiss the tip of her nose. As she closed her eyes and smiled, the photographer snapped the photo.

"That was the night you first told me you loved me," Vanessa said, taking the photo from his hand.

"I didn't think you would've kept the picture."

"Why not? I looked fabulous." She tried to laugh it off.

"Still."

"I asked Adriana to find some photos of us and put them up. For appearance's sake, that's all." She ushered him towards the door. "I'm going to change and do some reading. I'll see you at dinner."

"Okay." He waited until she closed the door before heading to his room down the hall. He sat down and pulled out his wallet. Behind the driver's license, he pulled out an identical photograph that was worn from the strokes over the years. Sighing, he looked up and said, "Oh Lord, what have you gotten me into?"

~ ~ ~

At their insistence, Phoebe joined the couple for dinner. As Carrie served the meal, Phoebe began asking questions. "So Andrew, it's my understanding that you run some sort of homeless shelter?"

"Not exactly, and please Ms. Carson, call me Andy." He looked up at Carrie. "If everything tastes as good as it smells, I'm going to enjoy myself. Thank you, Ms. Carrie."

The older woman was taken aback. She smiled. "You're very welcome, Mr. Andy."

"That will be all, Carrie," Phoebe said, eyes narrowing.

"Yes, ma'am." Carrie exited and Andy glanced at Vanessa who just shook her head slightly.

"Uh, I'd like to bless the food, if you don't mind."

"Not at all." Phoebe bowed her head but was startled when Andy took her hand and Vanessa's as well.

"Heavenly Father, thank You so much for this time that You have given us. We thank You for this new beginning for each of us, both individually and as a, well, family. Thank You for this abundance of food for which You have provided. Bless the hands that created and served it and bless those of us who will partake of it. In Jesus name we pray, Amen."

As they began to eat, Phoebe spoke. "When my niece came to me with the idea of marrying her college sweetheart in order to carry out the terms of her mother's will, I must admit I was a bit taken aback. I know she had many more——shall we say, suitable—— candidates that would have more than fit the bill. Especially since things did not end well between the two of you the first time."

Andy looked straight at Vanessa, who ducked her head. He turned to the older woman. "I was as surprised as you were, Mrs. Carson."

"It's Ms., but you may call me Phoebe, or Aunt Phoebe, if you prefer."

He nodded. "I never wanted to break up with Vanessa in the first place. But I guess she thought that my calling into ministry wasn't good enough. She

couldn't force me to give up my calling to fit into her
world."

"That's not true," Vanessa murmured.

"I guess my world was good enough for her after
all." He gave a small smile, but Vanessa turned away.

Phoebe shifted in her seat. "Yes, well, Vanessa was
young and didn't know her mind. As it turned out, the
two of you wound up together after all. Not in the most
ideal circumstances, mind you. But it is good for the
both of you, I suppose." She leaned in closer and
lowered her voice. "You do understand that no one
must get wind of the arrangement you have with
Vanessa. The scandal for our family would be
devastating."

"I do understand, Ms., Aunt Phoebe. And I promise
you, both of you, that I will do nothing to dishonor your
family or the foundation. I am just grateful to God that
He sent you when He did so that my kids won't wind up
back on the streets. The money that Vanessa pledged
to the mission will help in more ways than you can
imagine."

"I see. Well...then, that's good. As long as you treat
my niece well, I believe this arrangement will be
satisfactory. Don't you agree, Vanessa?" She glanced
over at the younger woman, who was busying herself
with the food on her plate. "Vanessa?"

"Hmm? Oh, yes, Aunt Phoebe?"

"I said, this arrangement between the two of you
will be satisfactory, don't you agree?"

"Oh, absolutely, Aunt Phoebe. Andy is one of the
most honorable men I've ever met. I couldn't be

happier that he agreed to help me out. Whatever the price we have to pay, it's a small one if it helps keep control of the foundation in our hands. And helps the mission," she added quickly.

"Good. Then that's settled." She turned back to Andy. "I hope you'll feel welcome here. This is your home for the next year, at least. Don't be afraid to live here. And you're welcome to have guests or other family come by." She stood. "Now, if you'll excuse me, I'll leave you two alone to get reacquainted."

"But you haven't eaten anything, Aunt Phoebe."

"I'll have Carrie bring something to my room. I feel it best that the first night of your marriage be spent together——alone. Good night."

"Well that was strange," Andy said.

"You have no idea," Vanessa replied. Her aunt had always been about proprietary standard and image. Yet, knowing that their marriage was one of convenience, Phoebe seemed to be encouraging them to turn it into something more. *How strange indeed.*

CHAPTER EIGHT

Survivial

The next morning, Andy started his day with devotion and a vigorous workout. Carrie had a bountiful breakfast spread waiting for him. "I didn't know what you liked, so I just made a little of everything. You let me know what your preference is and I'll have it ready for you every morning."

Andy shook his head. "I haven't had anyone make me breakfast since college. My mom would do it when I came home on the weekends. But after I graduated, she said I was on my own. I usually just grab some coffee and toast."

"Oh, that'll never do, Mr. Andy. That's why you're so skinny. You need to eat!"

"Now you really sound like my mother. The two of you would get along like gangbusters."

"I'm sure she's a fine woman, and I look forward to meeting her one day. But in the meantime, you sit down and eat."

"At least let me grab a shower."

"Fine. See you in ten minutes. I'll keep everything hot for you."

Andy ran upstairs, jumped in and out of the shower, changed into some sweats, and called his mom to check in. "You miss me?"

"I'm surviving," she said with a chuckle. "And how are you, mister newlywed?"

"I'm surviving. Vanessa's cook is downstairs and she's got enough food to feed a small army."

"I hope you're eating."

He couldn't help but laugh. "Yes, Mom, I'm on my way downstairs now to eat." He sighed. "I love you, Mom."

"I love you too, baby. I know this isn't the most ideal situation, but I really believe that God's going to work it all out. I feel it in my spirit."

"I wish I could."

"You just hold still and watch and see God work. In the meantime, you be nice to Vanessa——your wife."

"I will, I promise."

~ ~ ~

Andy was finishing his second cup of coffee when Vanessa joined him in the kitchen. "Good morning, Andy. Sleep well?"

He nodded. "That was the nicest mattress I have ever slept on. I didn't even think I was tired, but as soon as I lay down, it's like the pillows just swallowed me up and I was out! How about you?"

"I always sleep well in my own bed." She turned to Carrie. "Has Phoebe been up?"

"Yes ma'am. She was up and out early this morning."

"Did she say where she was going?"

"She didn't say and I didn't ask."

Vanessa shrugged. "We usually have breakfast together when I'm home. It's sort of a tradition."

Andy looked down at his nearly empty plate. "I'm sorry. I would have waited if I had known."

She waved him off. "It's okay. I don't expect you to keep my schedule." Carrie set a plate with eggs, bacon, an English muffin, and fruit in front of her. "Coffee, Miss Vanessa?"

"Yes, please. Thanks." She picked up her fork, and then glancing at Andy, quickly bowed her head and said a quick prayer. She began buttering her muffin. "So, what are your plans today?"

"Well, I have to go in to work today. With the infusion of cash, we've got to get some contractors lined up and arrange to get work done. Kendra is thrilled to be able to do a little shopping. More like an extreme makeover. By the way, in case I haven't said it before, thank you. I know why you're doing it, but the fact is, we would have had to shut down if you hadn't come along to help."

"You don't have to thank me, Andy. I'm glad to help. By the way, I've got several contractors that have done work for us that you should use."

"Thanks, but we've got people."

"Ex-cons?"

He frowned. "Why would you make that assumption?"

"Because, knowing you, you are a man of second chances."

"That's because I serve a God of second chances." He smiled. "We have a contractor who does hire ex-cons, yes. They're non-violent offenders who needed a break. But our guy has been with us a long time and he's done some great work for us, many times at his expense. I'd like to hire him and pay him for once, if you don't mind."

"Not at all. If you're sure he's the one you want, then do what you think is best. I just hope he's fair in his price."

"He's been more than fair, Vanessa. It's time I returned the favor." He finished off his juice. "So what are your plans today?"

"Nothing really." She took a bite of her fruit. "I've got some work to do for the foundation. Why?"

"I was just asking. I thought.... Well, I was just thinking maybe you'd like to come down and spend the day at the mission."

She frowned. "Why would I do that?"

"Because you are shelling out an awful lot of money to help us out. I figured you'd at least want to see what you're investing in."

"I don't know."

"It's not a bad idea, Miss Vanessa," Carrie added. Vanessa turned, but the older woman had turned away and was wiping the counter.

"It's okay," Andy said. "I just thought you might like to come. It would certainly help you to know more about what it is I do when people ask you what your husband does." He stood. "Thank you, Ms. Carrie for a lovely breakfast. Vanessa, I'll see you later." He picked up his breakfast dishes, but Carrie waved him off. He went over and planted a kiss on her cheek. She swatted him with a towel. Chuckling, he left the room, humming a tune.

Carrie came over and picked up Andy's breakfast dishes. "Now, I'm just saying, Miss Vanessa. It's probably not a bad idea for you to see where that young man is coming from. If you're going to be his wife, that is."

Vanessa scowled at the cook, but Carrie wasn't fazed. She simply took the dishes to the sink and hummed to herself.

~ ~ ~

Andy opened the door to his suite, surprised to see Vanessa standing there. "What's up?"

She tried not to gasp at the sight of Andy wearing nothing but a pair of pants. His lean frame was well defined. It was clear that working out over the years had paid off. Every inch of his torso and arms were chiseled almost to perfection. It was all she could do not reach out and touch him. *Steady girl. He's not the one.*

"Vanessa?"

She blinked, realizing that she had been ogling him for a full thirty seconds. "Um, yeah. I came up because I... I thought about it, and I decided I wanted you."

"Excuse me?"

"I mean, I wanted to be with you! No! I mean... Jesus!"

He laughed then reached over and rubbed her arm. "It's okay. Take a deep breath and start over."

She shook his hand off, but the goose bumps running up her spine wouldn't quit. "What I meant to say was that I wanted to go with you today. To the mission."

"Really?" He grinned. "That's great. What changed your mind?"

She folded her arms across her chest, pinching her inner arm to keep herself focused. "It's what you said. I'm spending a lot of money on you, I mean, your mission, and I should see where it's going for myself. Plus, as soon as people find out about our marriage, I know they'll want to know more about you and what you do. It would help if I could speak articulately about the place. Who knows? Maybe we'll be able to generate some extra donors."

"But what about your work?"

"It'll keep. Do you still want me along?"

"Of course."

"Good. I'll meet you downstairs in fifteen minutes."

He closed the door and she practically ran to her room. She slammed the door. *Get a grip on yourself, Vanessa. He's not into you. And you're not into him.*

This is strictly business. She felt her face flush. *Yeah, right.*

CHAPTER NINE

True to her word, fifteen minutes later Vanessa descended the stairs to find Andy waiting in the foyer. His smile turned into a frown. "What's wrong?"

"You're not wearing that, are you?"

"Why? What's wrong with it?" She glanced down. She was wearing a crisp, white linen pantsuit. She also sported a couple of diamond tennis bracelets with matching earrings and necklace. A couple of rings sparkled from her hands. Her jewel-encrusted black Prada bag matched her black and white Christian Louboutin heels.

"You can't go to the mission dressed like that."

"Why not?"

"What are you planning to do, sit around and have someone wait on you?"

"What were you expecting me to do?"

"To work. To help out. When I asked if you wanted to learn about the mission from the inside out, I assumed you would be getting involved. Volunteers don't come dressed like they're on a photo shoot. I mean, you look nice, but it's not really appropriate."

"So what do you suggest I wear?"

"Something comfortable. Jeans or khakis if you have them. And some comfortable shoes. You're going to be on your feet a lot and something tells me you won't be able to walk if you wear those."

She sighed. "Okay. Anything else?"

"Yes. Leave the jewelry behind. Earrings are okay and maybe a necklace and watch if you want. Something a bit less ostentatious."

"What kind of place is this?"

"These kids are coming in from the streets. It's hard for them to trust anyone and when they see someone like you coming in, dressed like you are now, their first impulse is to take what you have. Their second impulse is to try and denigrate you because they think you're only there because you feel sorry for them. They will abuse you to make them feel better about themselves. If you dress down, they'll feel a little more at ease with you."

"But you're in a tie."

"I'm the minister, remember? I'm also in charge. It conveys authority." He glanced at his watch. "Can you hurry? Our first group session is in 90 minutes."

"Okay, okay. I won't be long." She ran upstairs and ten minutes later, she was back downstairs in jeans and a cotton blouse, denim jacket and tennis shoes. She still had the Prada bag, but had taken off all the jewelry except for her earrings and her necklace. "Better?"

He tried not to snicker. "Much. Now let's get going."

They went out the front door to find Jackson standing on the side of a waiting Town Car. "What's this?"

"For us to get to the shelter."

Andy shook his head. "No way. I'm not going to show up in some fancy new car with those kids watching. Didn't we just have this conversation?"

"Well how do you suggest we get there, by bus?"

"No. But don't you have something a little less fancy?"

"There's a Range Rover and a Jag."

He groaned. Jackson spoke up. "There is your father's car, Miss."

Now it was her turn to groan. "That old thing? Will it even run?"

"Of course." Jackson was insulted. "All the cars in the garage are more than capable of going any distance."

"What kind of car is it?" Andy asked.

"It's a 1979 Buick Regal. He kept it in mint condition."

"That's perfect. Let's go."

"But Jackson can't drive us in that!" Vanessa cried.

"He's not driving us, I am. Lead the way, sir."

They followed Jackson to the garage. "I had the mechanic out to inspect the car just last month. She's good to go." He handed the keys to Andy without question and watched as they climbed in and drove off. "I'm sure that will be an interesting ride," he mumbled.

~ ~ ~

They pulled up in front of the mission just in time to witness several boys fighting. "Wait here," he instructed as he jumped out the car and ran over to start detangling the boys. As he did so, Vanessa gasped as he took a haymaker to the right side of his face. He didn't go down, but instead began pulling the boys apart, standing in between one boy and the other two. "Knock it off! Jabari, what's going on?"

The boy standing behind him said, "They took my watch! I want it back!"

"I ain't take yo stupid watch, nigga," one of the other boys yelled.

Jabari lunged for him, but Andy held him back. "You lyin'! I saw you with it!"

The third boy said, "Keyon didn't take the watch. Man, you need to step off fo' I break yo punk ass off." As he advanced, Andy held out his arm to stop him.

"That's enough! Keyon, you know the drill. Everything off." The boy grumbled, but grudgingly began emptying his pockets. He then took off his shoes, pants, and shirts, held out his arms, and turned around. "There. Satisfied?"

"Yes, thank you." As Keyon began putting his clothes on, he turned to the other boy. "You're next, Darien."

"Man, I ain't strippin' for you. Who you think you is?"

"I'm the man that's going to have you thrown in jail for assault and possibly theft. If you've got nothing to hide then you have nothing to lose. Let's go."

Darien swore. "I ain't take his watch."

"Then prove it."

"Man, I ain't doin' nothin'."

"C'mon, D," Keyon said. "Gon' and show this punk ass he was lyin'."

"That's enough of the language, Keyon. Darien, let's see it."

The boy shuffled around until Keyon punched him. "What'cha waitin' on, D? Just do like the man said!"

"No!"

Andy went over and began patting the boy down. Darien rolled his eyes as Andy pulled the missing watch from the waistband of the boy's jeans.

"I told you," Jabari shouted.

"No, you blamed it on Keyon. So, let's hear it fellas."

"Look, Rev," Keyon said, "I had the watch and I showed it to D. That's it. I didn't take it."

"Darien?"

"I ain't sayin' nothin'."

"Fine. You know the rules. If you're found with stolen property, you have to leave."

"What!"

"That's the rule. Since Keyon wasn't carrying it and he admits to touching it but not taking it, and you have it on you, I can only conclude that you stole the watch from Jabari. Get your things and leave. Now."

Darien uttered a string of profanities, cocked his fingers at both boys, and went inside. Andy turned to the other boys. "You're both on restriction and you've got extra cleanup chores for a week."

"But he took my watch," Jabari yelled.

"And he started swinging on us," Keyon countered.

"Both true. That's why you're both getting punished. Jabari, you know we don't settle anything by fighting. And Keyon, you had no business messing with Jabari's property. I don't know if you knew what Darien was up to, but you shouldn't have been fighting either."

"Man, I couldn't let him punk me, Rev!"

"You've got to learn, Keyon, there are other ways to settle issues other than by fighting. You keep this up and that pride and temper of yours will land you in jail or the morgue. Is that what you want, either of you?"

Both boys shook their heads. "Good. Now shake hands and get upstairs." The boys reluctantly shook hands and headed inside. Andy touched the side of his face where he had been hit as Vanessa jumped out of the car and ran to him. "Are you alright?"

"Nothing that an ice pack and some Advil won't help."

"Does this sort of thing happen often?"

"I've been hit harder, if that's what you mean."

"You can't be serious."

"Vanessa, these kids come to me after who knows what kind of home life and living on the streets. Sometimes, the only way they know how to communicate or protect themselves is through their fists. I'm," he gestured up at the building, "we're trying to change that. And if it means taking an occasional hit, so be it." He led her into the building and straight into his office. Kendra was waiting for him with an ice pack, a bottle of water, and a pack of Advil. "You saw?"

"Right down to the last punch. At least now you're holding your own," she said.

"You mean he's been seriously hurt?" Vanessa asked.

Kendra nodded. "One time, this kid got so mad at Andy he swung on him with a bike lock in his hand." Vanessa gasped. "Knocked him clean out."

"She really doesn't need to hear this, Kendra."

"I really do," Vanessa countered. "I can't take the chance on you getting seriously hurt, or worse."

"And screw up your deal, right?" Andy threw the ice pack down. "Look, I know what's at stake——for both of us. You don't have to worry. I can take care of myself. Kendra, please give Vanessa the nickel tour while I make some phone calls. And try not to share anymore horror stories, please?"

"Sure thing, boss," Kendra replied with a snicker. She turned to the other woman. "So what should I call you? Ms. Carson? Mrs. Perry? Mrs. Carson-Perry?"

"Vanessa will be fine." She turned to her husband. "Are you sure you're okay?"

"I'm fine. You two go on."

"Alrighty then," Kendra said. "Group in five."

He waited until they left before dropping his head down on his desk. "Oh God, help. This is going to be a long day." He smiled as he felt the joy of the Lord surrounding him. "They that wait on the Lord will renew their strength. Thank You, Lord." He sat up and picked up the phone and dialed his favorite handyman. "George? It's Andy Perry. Listen, remember that list of repairs that we needed to get done? Can you start right away? We've got the money to get whatever you need. Yes, I'm paying."

CHAPTER TEN

Keyon

Vanessa slipped her watch and rings into her pocket and plunged her hands into the hot, soapy water. Grabbing a sponge, she took the first pot and began scrubbing. Another hand reached into the water, startling her.

"You ain't got to do that," Keyon said. "That's my job."

"I don't mind."

"Nah, the Rev is making me do it." He waited until she moved out of the way before taking over. She took a seat and watched for several minutes.

"You were the young man fighting this morning."

Keyon shrugged. "Wasn't nothin'."

"You popped Andy in the face."

He chuckled. "Oh snap! You saw that?"

"I did."

"Man, that wasn't supposed to happen." He continued with the pans, rinsing them out and moving on to the next one quickly. "Rev is cool. I wasn't trying to hurt him. But that fool, Jabari? That's another story altogether." He rinsed out another pot, then turned to face her. "I ain't never seen you here before. How'd the Rev suck you into this place?"

"It's a long story."

"Uh-huh. You his old lady?"

Vanessa smiled. "Something like that."

"All right, Rev! I was beginning to think he was a monk or something. Maybe now he's gonna lighten up now that he's gettin' a little sumpin'-sumpin'." Seeing her frown, he held up his hands, laughing. "Whoa! I'm just kiddin' with you, miss."

"It's Vanessa."

"I'm kiddin' with you, Vanessa. By the way, I'm Keyon."

"It's nice to meet you, Keyon."

"You too." He nodded then turned back to his pots and pans.

She stood, picked up a towel, and began to dry the dishes. "How did you wind up here, if I may ask?"

He shrugged again. "I was runnin' the streets, doing my thang, y'know? It was hard, but I was makin' it. I heard about this place from a buddy of mine. It's pretty cool. The Rev is straight."

"What do you mean?"

"I mean, he's good people. He really looks out for us. He don't play favorites. His word is his word. First time in my life anybody was ever straight with me, know what I'm sayin'?"

She nodded. "Do you have family?"

"I ain't seen my daddy since I was little. My moms is somewhere. She had her issues. Couldn't keep a job, drinking, stuff like that. She was sick. We wound up living in our car. One day, she said she was going to find us some food. She never came back. I been on my own for about three years now. Doin' what I had to do, y'know?"

"So now you're here."

"Yup. Like I said, Rev was straight. He didn't judge, didn't try to shuffle me off to some foster home. He just let me stay here and get it together. He helped me get back in school."

"You like school?"

"It's alright. I'm taking classes in auto shop. I like fixing cars. Figure I could get through high school and learn to be a mechanic, get me a job, and get on my own for real."

"What about family?"

"Rev is helping me with that. I've got some of my momma's folks in Indiana. We're trying to hook up, work something out."

"Sounds good."

"Yeah, I guess it is." He rinsed out the sink and wiped his hands. "I'm done here. Gotta take out the trash. Nice meeting you, Vanessa."

"Same here, Keyon."

~ ~ ~

Vanessa was overwhelmed. By four, she was exhausted and had collapsed on the ratty couch in Andy's office. He smiled as she lay there, her hair hanging over her face. She probably had never worked this hard in her life. He brushed back her hair and she stirred. "You okay?"

She stretched then groaned. "The first thing you need to do is have Kendra order you some decent office furniture, including a comfortable couch." She sat up and stretched again.

"I've slept on it many times. It's not that bad."

"I'm amazed that you don't need a chiropractor."

"Couldn't afford one." He sat down next to her and began massaging her shoulders. "Rough day?"

"It was a bit much. But at least it's over."

He shook his head. "Not quite. Dinner has to be served, and there are evening intakes. My night shift supervisor is going to be late, so I have to stick around."

"For how long?"

"Until at least about eight. Can you hang with me?"

She shook her head. "I don't think so. I still have reading to do before my meeting tomorrow at the foundation. Can you take me home?"

"I can't. Kendra leaves in about an hour and I can't leave the place unsupervised. It'll take me more than ninety minutes to get you home and back again, especially in rush hour traffic."

"Fine. I'll call Jackson and have him come get me." She reached around then looked up. "My purse! It's gone! One of those delinquents must have taken it while I was sleeping."

Andy scowled. He stood and crossed over to the large file cabinet next to his desk. Unlocking it, he pulled her Prada bag out of the drawer. "You can relax. Kendra locked up your purse. We always keep our valuables locked away." He walked over and dropped it in her lap. "Now, if you'll excuse me, I have to go see if I can help some of the *delinquents* with their homework. I'll see you at home." He strode out of the office.

She swore, then pulled out her cell phone. "Jackson? I need you to come pick me up as soon as possible. I don't care what car you drive."

CHAPTER ELEVEN

Swimming

Andy arrived home around nine. He dropped his briefcase on the bench in the foyer and headed for the kitchen. Carrie greeted him. "It's about time you got here. I'll warm up your dinner."

"That's not necessary, Ms. Carrie. It's late, and you've got to be off the clock by now."

"Nonsense. Now sit down and I'll have something for you shortly." She turned her back to him and pulled out a few bowls from the refrigerator. She hummed as she put smothered pork chops, mashed potatoes with gravy, and a helping of mixed vegetables in a skillet. The smells made Andy's stomach growl. He blushed and she chuckled. In minutes, she laid everything neatly on a plate, along with a warm piece of cornbread with melted honey butter, and served it to him with a glass of milk.

As he blessed the food, she put the kettle on. "I always have a cup of chamomile tea at night. It helps me sleep. That and resting in the arms of Jesus." At his surprised expression, she laughed. "You think you're the only one who knows Jesus? Son, I've been knowing Him since before you were born. How else do you think I've survived this long?" She pointed a finger at him. "Before you ask, I'm not telling you my age." They shared a laugh. "So how did it go?"

"You mean at the mission? It was...awkward, which turned into disastrous." He ate another forkful of food before recounting the day's events starting with the wardrobe malfunction leading up to Vanessa's abrupt departure. "I don't even know why I was so upset with her. I guess it was her attitude. I expected better from her."

"Why? It's not like Miss Vanessa comes from the streets. She's lived a very privileged life. She doesn't understand the world you come from. And I'll bet you didn't spend any time trying to explain it to her, did you?"

He shrugged. "No, I suppose not. After we started out disagreeing about her choice of clothes and what car to drive, I just wanted a few minutes to meditate and focus on the day ahead. I turned on the radio and we drove in silence."

"And the first thing she witnesses is you wading into the middle of a fight. That's her first impression of the place and you did little to calm her nerves."

"Her nerves?"

"Yes. She was so disturbed, she came in and wouldn't eat a thing. She tried to work out but that didn't help. Finally, she started swimming laps." She nodded her head in the direction of the patio. "She's out there now."

He turned and looked outside the patio doors. The pool was illuminated but every few seconds, he'd see her form gliding to the end of the pool then turning and launching out towards the other end. "You think I should say something to her?"

"That's up to you, Mister Andy. Not my place to say." He turned, but she had moved to the sink and started humming again. He picked up his glass and walked outside. The water in the pool glowed and shimmered as Vanessa glided by. He couldn't help noticing her lithe body, toned arms gracefully slicing the water. She turned her head to catch a breath but the strokes were smooth and calm. He stood near the edge of the pool and waited. On her return lap, she looked up and rested her arms on the edge. "How long have you been standing there?"

"Not long. You look very good in there."

"Thanks. Is there something you wanted?"

"No. I mean, yes. I just wanted to see if you were okay."

"Like you care."

"Vanessa."

"Don't 'Vanessa' me, Andy. I had a really rough day and you didn't care."

"I did care. I do care."

"Is that so?"

"Yes."

"Did she send you out here?"

"Who, Carrie? No. Well not exactly."

"That's what I thought." She turned and launched into another set of laps. He called out to her but she wouldn't respond. He waited until she returned to his end of the pool, knelt down, and grabbed her arm, pulling her up. "What are you doing?"

"I want to talk to you, Vanessa."

"Yanking my arm and nearly drowning me is no way to get my attention."

He released her, but before she could swim away, he called out. "I'm sorry."

"For what?"

"For..." He rolled his eyes then looked at her. "I'm sorry for not taking your feelings into consideration. I should have warned you about the place and what you might encounter. It can be a bit overwhelming even for veterans like me. I shouldn't have been so sensitive. I should have realized that being at the mission would have taken you completely out of your comfort zone. And I should have made sure that you were okay. For all those things, I'm sorry. Will you forgive me?"

She wiped her wet hair out of her face. Her eyes narrowed as she tried to decide if he was sincere. "Okay. I accept your apology. But if you expect me to forgive you, there's something you'll have to do for me."

"What's that?"

"You'll have to throw me a birthday party."

"Sure. That's easy. I can get a cake and some flowers. I'll call my mom; she'll be happy to come out. And I'm sure Phoebe won't mind."

"I'm not talking a simple get together. I mean a party——Carson style."

"What does that mean?"

"We'll keep it simple, here at the house. Invite friends and family, members of the board."

"Is this formal?"

"Doesn't have to be. It'll also be a great opportunity to raise funds for the foundation and the mission."

"Wait, do I have to come?"

"Of course!"

"But I thought you wanted to keep our 'marriage' a secret."

"We will. As far as anyone is concerned, you're just a charity case for the foundation." He bristled at her characterization but kept quiet. "Don't worry. I'll take care of everything."

She climbed out of the pool. Her wet swimsuit clung to her every curve. Whoa, down boy. "Is there anything else?"

"Yes, there's one more thing." The next thing he knew, he was floundering in the water. He could hear her laughing all the way inside the house. *I suppose I deserved that. And it beats a cold shower.*

CHAPTER TWELVE

Party

Two weeks later, Andy stood in the foyer of the house waiting for the first guests to arrive. He tugged at the jacket of his new Armani suit. Vanessa insisted that he go shopping for a nice outfit for the party. They fought over how much should be spent. After all, if he was a struggling minister seeking funds for the mission, he couldn't come across looking like a picture from the pages of GQ. They settled on a tailored black suit matched with a purple and gray shirt and tie combination. He refused to purchase new shoes, instead opting to have his best black dress shoes shined to look new.

He heard the rustling of the catering staff putting the finishing touches on the place. Vanessa came rushing into the foyer trying to put her necklace on.

"Here, let me do that," he said. She sighed and turned around. He took the ends of the necklace and put them together. "There. All set."

She turned around smiling. "Thanks. You look great."

"So do you." She had chosen an elegant black sheath accentuated with a simple platinum and diamond necklace with matching earrings. A pair of strappy heels graced her ankles. "You don't think it's too much?"

"Well, it would be if we were doing this at my house. But for your friends? I'd call it understated elegance."

"Well said, sir." She slid her hands down the lapels of his suit jacket. "This was a great choice. I hope you're not too uncomfortable."

"It's fine."

She lingered a moment longer before saying, "I hope you're not too upset about keeping our arrangement a secret. It would cause more problems than I need right now."

"Same here. Not that anyone on the mission's board of directors would object, but it would certainly raise a few eyebrows at church."

"I'll just bet." She glanced at her watch. "Alright. The guests should be arriving at any moment. Why don't you go into the living room and turn on the music. I'll lead the first of the guests in and start the introductions."

"It's your party." He leaned over and kissed her on the cheek. "Happy birthday, Vanessa. I hope you have

fun tonight." He turned and left, not seeing the
growing grin on her face.

~ ~ ~

An hour later, Andy understood what political
candidates went through. He had been smiling since
the first guest arrived and had shaken every hand that
had been extended. He had told the story of the
Wentworth Street Mission at least twenty times. Pam
had served as his wingman, helping him navigate the
room and connect with the right people as Vanessa
mingled.

The good news was that he had received a few
generous checks to add to the mission's coffers, plus a
few "give me a call" responses for those who wanted to
discuss further how they could help Andy's efforts. He
was genuinely grateful for all the support he had
received. Several of the foundation's board members
had personally offered contributions. They also
encouraged him to resubmit the mission's application
for next year's funding.

As he leaned on the bar sipping his drink, he took
the time to admire his wife. Vanessa effortlessly
worked the room, making sure that each of her guests
had a few moments of her undivided attention. Many of
the older guests were friends of her parents' and she
wanted to be sure to pay them extra special attention.
Some of the younger crowd included friends that
Vanessa had made during her travels. It was a mixed
crowd of ages, genders, and races, but what made them
all connected was one thing——money.

Ella joined her son at the bar. "This is some crowd."

He gave her a hug. "I'm glad you could make it, Mom. It's good to see a familiar face. Can I get you something?"

"How about a white wine."

"You don't drink."

"Sure I do. On special occasions. And my daughter-in-law's birthday is a special occasion."

"Shhh! No one is supposed to know." He glanced around to make sure they hadn't been overheard. He signaled the bartender for a glass of wine for his mother. "You're sure you're okay with this?"

"Baby, I'm well over the legal drinking age. Besides, I'm only having one glass. And since that chauffeur of yours is driving me home, I don't have to worry about being incapacitated."

He smiled. "You're right. You should enjoy yourself if you want. There's lots of great food too."

"So I see. Far cry from the Sunday afternoon teas the women's groups throw at church. I don't see any tuna salad or frappe."

He chuckled. "I could go for something like that right now."

She laughed too. "You know, I've been talking with Phoebe. She's a very lovely woman, down to earth. She thinks the world of you." She leaned in closer and whispered, "I think she's hoping the two of you will stay together." Andy rolled his eyes at the suggestion.

Vanessa eased her way over. "Mrs. Perry, I'm so glad you were able to come."

"Thank you so much for inviting me, Vanessa. You have a lovely home."

"Thank you. Are you enjoying yourself? Can I get you anything?"

"I'm fine. I'm just catching up with Andy."

"Terrific." She frowned and Andy turned in her direction. An attractive couple came walking towards them. Vanessa excused herself and met them halfway. She greeted them warmly and steered them towards the center of the room.

"Wonder what that was about," Ella said.

"It's not important. What is important is that I find you a place to sit and grab a bite to eat."

CHAPTER THIRTEEN

Spill

It wasn't long before Andy found himself standing alone at the bar again. Once again, his eyes followed Vanessa as she worked the room. He noted how she took extra time with his mother, who was in a lengthy discussion with Aunt Phoebe. He smiled, wondering what the three of them found so interesting, especially when they turned in his direction and started laughing.

"So, you're the one."

He turned towards the speaker and found himself facing the gentleman that had made Vanessa so uncomfortable. "Excuse me?"

"You're the one she picked."

Andy frowned. "I'm not sure I know what you're talking about."

"Aw, come on now, bruh. I know all about your arrangement. Vanessa told me."

"Really. And you are?"

"Oh, I'm sorry. I'm Bryce. Bryce Harmon. Vanessa and I are very close friends. *Very close.*"

"Is that so? She never mentioned you." He stifled a grin when he saw the other man stiffen. "But then, Vanessa and I do like to keep a low profile. As part of our arrangement, we keep personal matters exactly that way——personal." He leaned in and lowered his tone. "And as her *very close* friend, I would think you would know better than to bring up personal business in this setting where anyone can overhear." He took a step back as the woman who had accompanied Bryce sidled up to him.

"Well, this certainly looks intense. Can a girl get a drink, or should I call security?"

Andy took a minute to size her up. She was shorter than Bryce by at least six inches, which she compensated for with 4-inch stilettos. She wore a knee length sleeveless black dress that hugged her voluptuous curves and showed just enough to make a man curious to want to know more. A stunning diamond tennis bracelet adorned her arm, accentuating the three-carat wedding band on her finger. She brushed back her shoulder length honey-accented hair and smiled. Andy knew a flirt when he saw one; he decided to play along. "No need. Bryce and I were just talking about all the lovely ladies in the room. Lo and behold, one of the loveliest of them all graces us with her presence."

"Umph, you are a charmer." She extended her hand, which he shook. "Regine Harmon."

"Andy Perry."

"So, you're Vanessa's new pet project." She laughed at his bemused expression. "She's always been known for helping those in need and I've heard people talking about the work you do. It's admirable."

"Thanks."

Bryce scowled as he draped his arm around his wife. "Oh babe, you've got it all wrong. Andy here is more than just Vanessa's newest pet; he's her husband."

"Husband?" Vanessa chortled. "Vanessa Carson finally tied the knot, huh? Well I'll be —"

"Watch your language. He's also a preacher."

"Is that so? Excuse me, Rev."

"It's just Andy."

"When did all this happen? And why didn't we know about it?"

Andy tried to hide his scowl. He knew Vanessa was going to be furious, but there was no way to wiggle out of it. "It's been a few weeks. We eloped and it was Vanessa's idea to wait until she could make a formal announcement in front of her family and friends. We thought her birthday party would be an ideal opportunity." He leaned over and said, "I'd appreciate it if you'd keep this between us. I'm sure since you're such good friends, it's okay, but I know she really wanted to surprise everyone."

"Your secret is safe with me." She turned to her husband. "Well, isn't that something?"

"It's something, alright." Bryce lifted his glass. "Congratulations."

"Yes, Andy, congratulations! We'll have to celebrate soon," Regine said.

"Of course. Excuse me." He went off in search of Vanessa.

Regine turned to her husband. "I'm surprised you didn't mention Vanessa getting married."

"It's like he said. It was a secret."

"But the two of you are so close. Surely you had to know."

"Yes, I knew. But it's like he said. It's a secret."

"Not anymore."

~ ~ ~

Vanessa paced the kitchen floor. "I can't believe you told."

"It wasn't me. It was your friend——your very close friend——Bryce something." He took her arm and stopped her in her tracks. "Is he the guy you told me about?"

She sighed. "Yes. It is. I didn't expect him to show up."

"Especially with his wife."

"No." He released her and she continued to pace.

"Does she know about the two of you?"

"Maybe. I don't know."

"If she does, she's going to be a problem——for both of us."

"What are you suggesting?"

"We beat her to the punch."

~ ~ ~

"Are you sure about this?"

"About as sure as I was when I let you talk me into this in the first place." He smiled.

"Then let's do it." Vanessa turned to the crowd, took a fork, and tapped the side of her champagne flute. "May I have your attention please?" She looked over at Andy, who winked. As everyone turned to face her, she began. "I owe all of you an apology. It seems that I brought you here under false pretenses." As the crowd murmured, she continued. "Yes, this is a party celebrating my birthday. And yes, I wanted you to meet Andy and help raise funds for his ministry. However, there's more to the story." She could see Pam surreptitiously shaking her head, but she ignored her. "You see, Andy and I were college sweethearts once upon a time. We went our separate ways, but, through a stroke of fate——or as Andy might say, through a stroke of faith——we were brought together again. As it turned out, our feelings never really died. And before I knew it, he proposed, I accepted, and we got married!" She and Andy laughed as the room erupted into cheers. Many of those gathered came up to the couple and offered their congratulations, peppering them with questions.

Another tap of a champagne flute, and everyone turned to the rear. Regine had lifted her glass and said, "Well, since we seem to be at an impromptu wedding celebration, it's only fitting that we offer up a toast. To Vanessa and Andy, may you have a long and happy life together!"

"To Vanessa and Andy!" the guests chorused. Everyone raised their glasses and drank. Everyone except Bryce.

~ ~ ~

"That went better than I expected," Vanessa said, in between bites of her birthday cake. She sat at the kitchen counter while Andy fixed himself a sandwich and a glass of milk.

"Considering the circumstances, I'm amazed that it took this long before anyone found out." He sat down across from her. "Why did you tell Bryce about our arrangement and then invite him to the party?"

"He knew about the terms of my mother's will. I told him about that and he understood. I didn't think he'd show up, much less open his mouth."

"If he's going to present a problem..."

"He won't. I'll make sure of it." Just then the phone rang. "I'll get it." She got up and grabbed the cordless phone on the counter. A brief conversation ensued then she sat down. "That was Pam."

"She still angry?"

"Only a little. She said it's the second time we've blindsided her and if we do it again, she's quitting."

"Is she serious?"

"No. She's my best friend. She'll get over it."

"So, what did she want?"

"She's been getting calls from several media outlets about our marriage. They want interviews with us."

"Do you think it's a good idea?"

"Pam thinks so. We can tell our story our way. It'll keep the speculation down. Look at it this way: it'll be good publicity for the mission."

"I told you I don't want those kids to be exploited. They've been through enough."

"Fair enough. We'll make sure that we can veto any part of the story that would be detrimental to the mission or the kids. Deal?"

He thought a few moments. "Okay, deal. I guess we'd better get our story straight."

CHAPTER FOURTEEN

Sparks

A week later, Pam went around the house, checking the staging of each room on the first floor. The photographer was on his way over to take some establishing shots of the house prior to the interview. Pam had secured a few photos from Andy's room and had placed them around the home. Along with the staff, she'd ensured that everything was spic and span.

Vanessa and Andy came downstairs; Pam gave them a smile of approval. Wanting to appear comfortable rather than formal, Vanessa had opted to wear a simple purple pantsuit, accented with silver earrings and a diamond tennis bracelet. Andy kept it simple with a solid black shirt and slacks.

Pam could see the tension radiating from Andy. She went over and gripped his shoulders. "Relax, Andy.

We've gone over all this. Stick to the story, and you'll be fine."

"What if they ask something we haven't prepped for?"

Vanessa wrapped her arm in his. "Don't worry, I'll handle it." She smiled. "You just look at me like you're crazy about me." She leaned in and gave him a kiss on his cheek.

"I'll do my best."

~ ~ ~

Andy sat in the living room fiddling with his newly purchased wedding ring. When they decided to get married, they had agreed to avoid wearing rings. But since their picture was being taken, Pam decided it was better if they wore the appropriate jewelry. Fortunately, because they were supposed to have bought rings on the spur of the moment, Andy was able to get away with a simple gold band. Vanessa picked out a modest diamond wedding band that would complement Andy's financial status but didn't look too inexpensive.

Vanessa's background was already public. The reporter from Ebony had done some background homework on Andy, having spoken to his mother and Kendra. "So now I understand the two of you dated in college," the reported said. "Why did you break things off?"

Vanessa smiled. "That was me. I just wasn't ready to settle down. I loved Andy so much, but I wasn't ready to commit. Blame it on immaturity."

"It was hard on both of us," Andy added. "But in the end it was probably for the best. I wanted to go to graduate school and start the ministry. I couldn't have been the committed husband Vanessa deserved. It wouldn't have been fair to either of us."

"I see," said the reporter. "How is it that you two came back together?"

"A twist of faith," Andy said with a grin.

"Faith?"

"Yes. The mission was in dire need of a new source of funding. Kendra, my assistant, made the choice to contact the Carson Foundation without my knowledge. That led to a lunch meeting with Vanessa, which led to dinner, which led to here!" *Well, that's the truth.*

"I couldn't believe I was meeting with Andy," Vanessa added. "When I saw him, all those feelings came rushing back. I just knew he was the right one for me."

"So why did you elope?"

"I didn't want to take the chance of letting her get away again," Andy replied. "I let her go once and it took me ten years to get her back. No way was I going to let that happen again." *Not that I had a choice.*

"Vanessa, I know you've been linked with several eligible men in the past, but you never settled down. Why now?"

"As you know, I spent the better part of the last year caring for my mother. As we spent time together, we talked a lot about my father and their relationship. She always said that theirs was a once-in-a-lifetime love. The more she talked about it, the more I wanted that for myself. I began praying and asking for that same kind of love to come my way. Then Andy reentered my life. He was the answer to my prayers." *Okay, I know God's gonna get me for this one.*

"You talked about prayer. Does your faith play a part in your relationship?"

"Absolutely," Andy answered. "Our prayer is to take each day one at a time. We're still learning each other and it's not always easy. We are also learning how to balance our outside lives with our private lives. So prayer helps to keep the channels open, not just with God, but with each other. Plus, ours is a living faith. We use each of the avenues of our work——me through the mission and Vanessa through the foundation——to model after the Scripture in James that says, Faith without works is dead. That's one of the reasons that I hadn't settled down. I needed a wife who understood the importance of this ministry. Vanessa is the perfect partner for me because her work through the Carson Foundation is so vitally important. I'm so grateful that I have her in my life." He reached over and brushed his hand gently across her cheek before leaning over and kissing her.

It was just enough of a kiss to send shivers down Vanessa's body. Taking his hand, she kissed him back. She would have continued, but Pam, standing in the background, cleared her throat. Vanessa pulled back, but not before running her hand across his head. Smiling, she turned back to the reporter. "I'm sorry. That was rude. You know how it is with newlyweds."

"No need to apologize," the reporter said. "It's wonderful when you can witness real love in front of your eyes." She checked her watch. "I should get going anyway. I need to get back to my office and file my notes." Everyone stood and shook hands. "Andy, I'll look forward to meeting you at the mission next week. Thank you for taking the time to meet with me. This is going to be a great story." Pam escorted the reporter to the door then came back in.

"Well kids, you pulled it off! I think this will pass the smell test." Pam turned to Andy. "After they take photos at the mission, she'll probably sit down with Kendra and some of the kids."

"I told you I don't want them to be exploited."

"They won't. We're just going to ask them some questions about how the mission has helped them. We'll fold it in to show the work that you've been doing has made a real difference in these kids' lives. And if they don't want to be interviewed or photographed, they won't be. By the way, nice touch with the kiss. If I didn't know better, I'd swear it was real." She patted him on the back. "I'll see you on Monday, Andy. Vanessa, I'll be in touch." She turned to go, but then turned back to them. "Andy, you should probably be prepared. After this article comes out, so will the paparazzi. They will probably be following your every move, so watch your step. We'll talk more on how to deal with them. Have a good evening, kids."

The two of them stood staring at each other, unsure of what to do next. Finally, Andy said, "That wasn't as bad as I thought it would be."

"Good. I'm glad. I hope you weren't too uncomfortable telling that story. I know you're not much of a fan for lying."

"That's the thing. It wasn't really a lie. Everything happened the way I said it did. I'm not obligated to share the details of our arrangement with anyone. When people ask me how this all came about, I can tell them the exact same story and not feel guilty in the least. It's easier to tell people the truth they want to hear rather than all the details anyway. Besides, it makes a very romantic story." He had another thought. "What about your mother's will? What if someone goes digging and learns about the codicil?"

"The contents of the will have been sealed. It would take a court order to open the records. No one is going to find out unless someone who already knows blabs. Our attorney is bound by his oath and Aunt Phoebe would die before she breathed a word of this to anyone."

"My mother isn't one to gossip so we don't have to worry about her. Kendra is too protective of me to say anything. What about Bryce and Regine?"

"Bryce will keep quiet. I don't think Regine knows and if she does, I doubt if she'll say anything. Bryce will make sure of that."

"Then we're good. Now I just have to get through Monday."

"You'll be fine."

"I'm glad you think so." He checked his watch. "I'd better get upstairs and go over my notes for this weekend's service."

As he turned away, she called out to him. "Can I ask you something?"

He turned back. "Sure. Shoot."

"Why did you kiss me?"

He shrugged. "I don't know. It just seemed right. I mean, like the right thing to do. For the interview," he added.

"I see. You're probably right. Good call."

He went upstairs. She shrugged off her disappointment and went into the study to call Bryce.

CHAPTER FIFTEEN

Serpentine

"I don't like it."

"What don't you like, Kendra?" Andy asked, not looking up from his notes.

"The reporter and photographer being here. The way they are sniffing around trying to get some dirt on you and Vanessa."

"They're here to do a story about the mission. Any publicity we get that leads to donations is a good thing."

"Maybe. But I still don't like it."

"You'll be famous."

"If I wanted to be famous, do you think I'd be working here?" She stood in front of his desk, hands on her hips. "We're supposed to be doing the Lord's work, not providing fodder for the tabloids."

"We are doing the Lord's work. The work hasn't changed just because we're getting some notoriety. It just makes what we do more critical as those who need us most will be seeking us out for help. Now we'll have the resources to provide help. Look at it this way: even Jesus had to deal with fame."

"Uh-huh, and look what happened to him."

He started to laugh until he looked up at her face and saw how serious she was. He stood, came around the desk, and wrapped an arm around her shoulders. "It'll be fine, I promise. After the story comes out, we'll deal with what comes and we'll fade into oblivion again. And remember, this is all your fault."

"My fault!"

"Yes. You applied to the Carson Foundation, remember?" He couldn't suppress a grin as she punched him in the side. "Ow. That almost hurt." He laughed as she stormed out of his office into hers. He chuckled as he headed back to his desk. Looking at the stack of bills on his desk, he thanked the Lord that, for the first time, there was enough money in the bank to pay them and plenty left over. He decided to add a second check with his handyman's invoice. George had never given Andy a bill; he simply said, "Give me what you can." Andy knew his paltry offering——when there was one——wasn't nearly enough to cover parts and labor. This way, George could begin to recoup some of his earnings. Andy prayed that George would be blessed by this extra bonus.

"Knock, knock."

He looked up and smiled in surprise. "Regine! What are you doing here?"

"Looking for a little help."

"What kind of help?"

"I've got a donation for your mission and I need a little help bringing it in. It's outside in my truck."

"Sure thing." He stood and went over and shook her hand. "This is definitely a surprise."

"I know. Since we met, I've been thinking about you and the mission and wondered how I could help. I know I could've written a check, but I wanted to do something more tangible. So I did what I do best——I went shopping."

Andy followed Regine outside, expecting to see an SUV. There was a U-Haul truck instead. "What's all this?"

"Supplies for your kids. I didn't know what all was needed so I brought some of everything——laptops, printers, linens, toiletries, cleaning supplies, diapers, baby clothes, whatever. Wal-Mart and Target are terrific places to shop."

Even though she was dressed in jeans and a blouse, the silver and platinum dripping from her ears, neck, and fingers along with a pair of Manolo Blahnik heels and matching bag betrayed her attempt at humility. "You shop at Wal-Mart?"

"Cleaned them out, sweetie! Best deals for your money and if I'm going to spend it, I want all I can get for it."

"Wow!" He surveyed the entire truck. "I'm going to need some help. I'll get some of the kids to help." He smacked his hand to his head. "Wait, I've got that reporter from Ebony inside interviewing the kids."

"I didn't realize. If this is a bad time..."

"No, it'll be fine."

"Andy, I hope you know I didn't show up today expecting publicity. In fact, I'd really appreciate it if you kept my name and photo out of this."

"Shouldn't be a problem. But do you mind if the photographers took photos of the kids bringing in the stuff?"

"Not at all."

Kendra emerged outside. "Andy, the reporter wants to talk to you." She surveyed the truck. "What's all this? Where did it come from?"

"From a very generous benefactor. Regine Harmon, I'd like you to meet my deputy director and right-hand woman, Kendra Rollins. Kendra, this is Regine Harmon. She's a friend of Vanessa's who wanted to help out."

Regine squeezed Andy's shoulders. "I hope I'm a friend of yours as well."

"Of course!"

Kendra frowned but extended a hand. "Very nice to meet you, Ms. Harmon."

"Please, call me Regine."

She nodded. "Andy, the reporter?"

"Yeah, that's right. Kendra, can you round up some of the kids and get them to help unload this stuff? We'll put it in the community room and deal with inventory later."

"Since this is my doing," Regine began, "why don't you let me handle the inventory? I'm not even sure of everything I bought. I can sort out the whole thing and help you distribute it where it needs to go."

"That would be great, Regine. As soon as I'm done with the reporter, I'll come and give you guys a hand." He hurried inside.

Regine smiled and turned to Kendra. "So you've known Andy a long time?"

"Yes, I have. We've been together since the start of the mission. I have his back at all times."

"I'll just best you do. It's good that he has someone like you to watch over him." She glanced around. "Can you show me where I should go?"

"Of course. Right this way." *I'll show you exactly where you should go. No, sir. I don't like this one bit.*

CHAPTER SIXTEEN

Suspicious

A week later, Andy greeted his pastor, Reverend Fred Dillon, and one of the members of the mission's board of directors, Evelyn Freeman, in his office. They had asked for an informal meeting to discuss the recent changes.

"I like what you've done with the place," Pastor Dillon said.

Andy studied Sis. Freeman. The woman wore a perpetual scowl on her face, as if her girdle was too tight. She stood in her too-tight polyester suit, buttoned to the top, her feet squeezed into heels that had to be a half-size too small. Her wig sat perched atop her head, covered by one of her many church hats that she refused to be seen without. As she glanced around the room, she sniffed, each time making the hat bobble on her head.

Vanessa had insisted he upgrade his office furniture. The decade-old sofa had been replaced with a new microfiber one. His used desk and bookshelves had also been upgraded. "Vanessa thought we could use some improvements around here. She wanted to go really high-end, but I insisted on more modest purchases." He offered them a seat on the couch and pulled up one of the new task chairs.

"It's just fine, fine," Dillon said. "I hope I'll be blessed enough to make some upgrades to my office soon."

Andy blanched. He suddenly felt embarrassed by his surroundings, something he was completely unaccustomed to feeling. "So, what brings you both by?"

"We just wanted to check up on you and see how things were going," Sis. Freeman said. "With all the news surrounding the mission, we just thought it appropriate to come by and encourage you."

You came by to get the dirt. He silently prayed for forgiveness. These people had supported the mission since the beginning and had a right to be concerned about its status. "I know a lot has happened in the last few weeks, and I apologize for not sitting down with the board sooner. I hope you are pleased with the upgrades to the facility. It's made a world of difference in the kids' lives."

"Uh-huh," Sister Freeman said. She was one of the church's trustees, in charge of beautification. Andy knew that she was more annoyed that she had not been consulted about the changes. He also knew she was a notorious gossip. "So I guess your wife is making all the decisions now."

"Not at all. She did make some suggestions for the office furniture and paint, but the rest of the decisions were Kendra's and mine. We took suggestions from the staff and volunteers as to what was needed most and with our new funding, and we were able to do those things we always wanted to do but had to put off because of lack of money."

"I see. I suppose your wife will have more to say about how we upkeep the church."

"I don't think so, Sister Freeman."

"Not that I'd mind suggestions. She does have lovely taste." She ran her hand across the fabric of the couch. "And with an increase in our church finances, I'm sure we'd be able to make some improvements that would be up to standard."

Before Andy could respond, Pastor Dillon asked, "Speaking of your wife, I was surprised that you didn't come to me before you decided to get married."

"Is there something wrong?" Andy asked.

"Oh no, no. I just believed that you always wanted to marry in the church. And that you'd seek out premarital counseling."

Andy sucked on his teeth. "I know this was a shock to you, Pastor. And if I felt that I needed to come to you about this, I would have sought your counsel. However, I believe that God brought Vanessa and me together. We're very happy and we're working through the adjustment of living as a couple."

"Counseling would have helped prepare you both."

"Maybe. But I look at our relationship the way the Bible showed us relationships. In the Old Testament, couples didn't seek counseling. In fact, quite often, they married without even knowing each other. Look at Isaac and Rebekah. Jacob and Rachel. Ruth and Boaz. Marriages were as much about business as they were about love. Yet when God drew them together, their marriages lasted because God sustained them. I believe that will happen with us."

"And just when are you going to introduce your bride to the church?" Sis. Freeman asked.

"She's been there already. I've introduced her to a few people. She didn't want to call attention to herself as she came to worship." He let that zinger soak in before speaking again. "Rest assured, I will be introducing her to everyone now that our news has been made public. Is there anything else? Any other questions I can answer for you?"

"There has been discussion among some of the board and the membership," Rev. Dillon said.

"Regarding?"

"Simply put, many are asking since you have a new source of income, should the church's financial contribution be redirected elsewhere?" Sis. Freeman asked.

"I can't answer that, Sis. Freeman."

"Can't or won't?"

"Are you accusing me of some sort of impropriety?"

Rev. Dillon waved his hands. "Not at all, Andy. The thinking was that because our contribution has been so meager, it may not be needed any longer."

"Pastor, the contributions of the church are always welcome. But I understand your concerns and I'm well aware of the church's financial state. I would be happy to bring the mission's books to the board meeting next month. The members are welcome to examine them and if they feel that church is unwilling or unable to contribute any longer, so be it.

"But I would add that the church's contributions have been more than just financial. This mission was built out of the prayers and volunteers of the church members who believed in what we were doing here for these kids. Over the years, they have come through with donations of food and clothing, but more important, of time. Even if the church stops giving money, I hope the members will continue to give of their time and energy. The financial blessing we have received here will do more than just help the kids. We are finally in the position to hire staff members, full and part-time. My hope is that some of those positions can be filled with qualified members of our congregation."

Rev. Dillon perked up at this bit of news. "Praise the Lord! Oh, that's a fine idea, Andy, just fine! It's wonderful when you can bless those who have supported you all these years." He stood. "We should get out of your way now. Sis. Freeman?"

She didn't seem as eager to move, but not wanting to disrespect her pastor, she stood. "I'll look forward to meeting your wife on Sunday, Andy. Perhaps the two of you would be willing to participate in a gathering in your honor."

"That's not necessary, Sis. Freeman."

"It's the least we can do, since we weren't invited to your wedding. Think of it as a reception. It'll just be cake and punch in the fellowship hall after service. I'll take care of everything." She turned and walked out the door before he could respond.

Andy groaned. "Pastor..."

"I'll talk to her, Andy. But you know how she gets." The two men shook hands. Andy waited until he was alone before collapsing in his seat. He shook his head. Vanessa was going to kill him.

~ ~ ~

Vanessa was a good sport about the "reception." Andy's mother agreed to run interference with any of the good "sisters," should they begin to pry too deeply into the couple's business. When Sis. Freeman cornered Vanessa and inquired about how she and Andy got together, Vanessa repeated the same story they had told to the reporter. That seemed to mollify Sis. Freeman's inquiries, but she had one more question. "When will you be moving your membership?"

"Excuse me?"

"I just thought since you and Rev. Perry were married now, you'd be joining our church body. Once we know when you'll be coming along, we'll be able to include you in some of the women's ministry activities."

Before Vanessa could respond, Andy came and sat by her side. "How're we doing over here, ladies?"

"Just fine, sweetie. Sis. Freeman was just inquiring about when I planned to move my membership to your church." She raised her eyebrows, indicating this was his problem.

"Vanessa is a member of her own church. She hasn't decided if she's going to be a part of our church."

"Well, of course she is. It just wouldn't do if you and your wife were worshipping at separate congregations. It just wouldn't look right."

"While I agree with you in principle, there's nothing that says we have to attend the same church," Andy replied.

"The Bible says a house divided against itself cannot stand. Mark 3:25."

"True. But nowhere does it say that the wife has to join her husband's church. Perhaps it should be that the husband follows the wife. Or maybe they both attend the church that the Lord leads them to. Perhaps we'll leave our respective churches and start our own. Either way, I know we'll have your blessing, won't we, Sis. Freeman?"

Sis. Freeman looked sick. She began fanning herself with enough speed to blow the curls of her wig back under her hat. "Yes, yes of course. Won't you excuse me?" She stood and walked over to another table where several of the church mothers had gathered.

"That wasn't very nice, Andy," Vanessa said.

"Depends on your idea of nice. All she wanted was to get into your business. It's none of her business what

church you attend. All Sis. Freeman does is start mess."
He surreptitiously pointed at the woman's back. "Right
now, she's over there telling the mother's board that
you have somehow corrupted me and turned me into a
downright rude young man."

"Really? How is that my fault?"

"It's not. Sis. Freeman has never been a fan of mine.
She's always thought of me as rude, even more so since
I'm always disagreeing with her at our board
meetings."

"If she's that much trouble, how did she wind up on
the board?"

"She's on the board of trustees here at the church.
Since the mission was originally founded as part of the
church, I needed a representative from the trustee
board to serve on my board of directors. No one really
wanted to do it, so Sis. Freeman appointed herself.
She's harmless for the most part, except for her
mouth."

"Now you know why I'm so selective with my
friends. You never know who's going to take something
you say and run to the nearest tabloid. People like that
are dangerous."

Ella Perry slipped in next to them. "Andy, what's
this I hear about you starting your own church?"

"What?"

"Word is spreading like wildfire. Sis. Freeman said
she heard it straight from you."

Andy and Vanessa burst out laughing. "I told you
so," they said simultaneously.

"What's so funny?"

"I'll let Vanessa tell you. Right now, I better go catch Pastor Dillon and have a word with him before he gets wind of this." He shook his head. "The more things change, the more they stay the same." He kissed his wife and mother on their cheeks and excused himself.

CHAPTER SEVENTEEN

Escape

"This is getting ridiculous." Andy slammed the paper down on the kitchen counter where Vanessa was having a cup of coffee. "It's bad enough I let you talk me into that interview and the profile at the mission. Now they're just digging up dirt and making stuff up as they go along." He pointed to the newspaper columnist's blurb about Andy supposedly using his mission to start a teen cult. "Where do they get this stuff?"

"It's all part of people's fascination with the seamier side of life. Anything they can dig up on a famous person, they'll use it. And if they can't dig it up, they'll make it up."

"But I'm not famous."

"You are by proxy because of me." She rubbed his arm. "I'm sorry I dragged you into this mess. You don't deserve this kind of headache."

He sat down and sighed. "The worst part is that they're starting to bug my mother. They're at her house, following her to the grocery store, and now they're starting to pester her at work. Somehow, they got a list of her coworkers' names and they're going after them."

"I'm so sorry, Andy."

"I didn't sign up for all this and neither did my mom. She may have to take a leave of absence; but then I don't want her to become a virtual prisoner in her own home."

"She could come stay here with us. That would give her some sense of privacy."

"She won't hear of it."

"What about bodyguards?"

He shook his head. "That would be worse."

Vanessa grabbed her cell phone and put in a call to her publicist. "Pam? It's Vanessa. Yes, I know about the article. Andy brought it to me. Listen, Andy's mom is getting harassed by the press. I thought we made it clear that she was off limits? Okay, you do whatever you have to do to get them to back off. I mean it. Not another reporter in her face, at her home, or her job. If her name so much as shows up in somebody's birthday column, they're done, is that clear? Same goes for Andy's church and the mission. Let them know if they print any unauthorized or damaging articles, they're going to get hit with the most massive lawsuit in history. And if they're not scared of that, they can expect to be bought up and torn down in a heartbeat. Clear? Thanks."

Andy's mouth hung open. "You can do that? Just order the press to knock it off?"

"I can't. Pam can. She's connected with the right people. The Carson Foundation, me in particular, makes for good copy. They do not want to be shut out of our media machine. Plus, my lawyers are very, very good."

"Wow. I'll bet there are a lot of celebrities who'd pay to have your kind of power over the press."

"No, they wouldn't. Contrary to popular belief, they need the press. They may not like the tabloid aspect of it and certainly none of them need the paparazzi climbing all over them. But press, even not-so-flattering press, keeps them out there. It keeps their names in the public eye and that's exactly what they need when it comes time for them to push their next movie or CD. When the tabloids print those negative stories, it only makes the public more sympathetic. If the mainstream turns on you, look out."

"I don't know how true that is, but I thank you just the same for putting the word out about my mom and the mission. I really appreciate it."

"It's no problem." She drank her coffee and watched as he snacked on an apple.

"What?"

"I was just thinking."

"About?"

"One of the ways to get the press off our backs is to disappear for a while."

"Rehab?"

She laughed. "No, silly. I was thinking of a vacation."

"Now?"

"Yes. It would be a perfect time to get away. A delayed honeymoon."

"I don't know."

"C'mon, it'll be fun. We can relax, get away from everything for a few days. Pam will work her magic with the press while we escape. You know you need the break. I certainly do. It's been a grueling couple of months for me, Andy."

"Then you should go."

"And have the press speculating about us taking separate vacations? If you thought it was bad, it will be ten times worse. Please, Andy. Don't make me beg."

He bit into his apple and thought. He could see her point. He couldn't remember the last time he had gone on a vacation. Plus, in the last few months, Vanessa had gone from losing her surviving parent to running the foundation to being married and caught in the eye of a media storm. It hadn't been easier on him with the press harassing him and catching flak from the church. "Okay. Give me a week to make sure things are covered at the mission and we'll go. Where are we going?"

"You'll see. I'll take care of all the arrangements," she replied, grinning.

~ ~ ~

Vanessa chose a secluded island spot in the West Indies. From the moment they arrived, it was clear that she was a frequent visitor, greeted warmly by the staff. The manager led them from the main lodge to their individual cottage, just steps away from the pristine pink and white sandy beach. To his credit, the manager didn't question Vanessa's marital status or the fact that she had opted for a two-bedroom villa. He simply welcomed them and reminded them that if they needed anything, to feel free to contact him personally.

Andy started to unpack but Vanessa stopped him. "The staff will take care of that," she explained. "Why don't you get changed and I'll give you a tour of the place." Ten minutes later he emerged, changed into a comfortable shorts set and she in a lightweight multi-colored sundress and wide-brimmed sun hat. She handed him a straw-colored hat. "The sun can be pretty intense these first few days. You'll need it."

They stepped out on the patio and took in the scene. Except for their footprints, the sand on the beach was undisturbed. The only sounds were the gentle breeze blowing through the trees and the sounds of the Atlantic lapping against the shoreline. In the distance, he could hear the strains of a steel drum band, performing at the main lodge. "A friend of mine told me about this place. It's absolutely gorgeous. You can let yourself go without fear of anyone taking photographs or having reporters asking questions. The only people on this part of the island are guests and staff and they are discreet."

They began their walk near the shore. Andy marveled at the stark colors of the sand versus the crystal blue water. He had never seen anything quite like it. Vanessa took off her sandals and ran to the edge of the water, allowing the coolness of the ocean to soothe her feet, singed by the hot sand. She tipped her head back slightly, letting the sun's warmth caress her skin. "I brought my mom here right after we found out about her diagnosis. I thought it was important that she find some peace and quiet before she began focusing on her treatment. We spent the days just walking and talking along the beach. I tried to get her to go windsurfing with me, but she wasn't having it."

"I'll bet she enjoyed this beach. It's gorgeous," he replied. He had pulled off his sandals and stood next to her, gazing out at the ocean.

"She did. I took lots of pictures and when she was going through chemo, she would leaf through the album. She said it helped keep her spirits up." She didn't say anything else, choosing to stare off into the horizon.

Andy put his arm around her shoulders. "You were a good daughter, Vanessa. You gave her some wonderful memories. No one could have asked for more." He squeezed her gently as he heard her sniff. She leaned into him, letting him comfort her until she was more at ease. They continued their walk. The beach was deserted and for Andy, the quiet was a little unsettling. He was so used to the sounds of the city; he never imagined that there could be any place with so little noise. "So besides soaking up some sun and windsurfing, what else is there to do?"

"There's all types of water sports. You can do some fishing if you like. And there are tours around the island."

"My mother would love this place."

"We should bring her down next time."

He grinned. "Next time? Is there going to be a next time?"

"Maybe. Maybe not." Her smile was coy. "We'll just have to wait and see. Come on. Let's head to the main house. We're just in time for an early supper."

They walked to the building, still joined together. It felt comfortable and familiar and neither wanted the feeling to end. As they reached the restaurant, the host seated them at a cozy table near the window with a view of the ocean. They ordered the chef's special with a bottle of wine. They chatted about whatever topics came to mind and if there were any disagreements, they moved on, not willing to spoil the atmosphere.

The dessert came. Vanessa reached over and took her husband's hand. "This has been one of the best evenings of my life. Thank you so much. I really needed it."

He lifted her hand to his mouth and kissed it. "I'm glad we came too. As much as I've enjoyed the food, I've enjoyed the company even more." He kissed her hand again and looked over at her. The desire in her eyes clearly matched what he was feeling. "Vanessa——"

The waiter interrupted him. "May I get you anything else?"

"No, thank you."

"Was everything to your satisfaction?"

"Most definitely," Vanessa responded. "Thank you so much."

"It was my pleasure. I'll leave you to your desserts." He nodded at them before departing.

Andy started to speak but she stopped him. "Why don't we go back to the cabin? We can talk about...everything."

He nodded and stood, holding her hand and helping her to ease out of her seat. She started to walk away but he pulled her close, drawing her in for a slow, lingering kiss that left them both breathless. "Let's go." They drew together, arms locked. He raised up her hand again, this time kissing her wrist, sending shivers all over her body.

"Of all the gin joints in all the world, as they say."

The couple turned, startled to see Bryce and Regine coming toward them. Andy immediately stiffened and released his hold on Vanessa. "Bryce, Regine. This is certainly a surprise," she managed to say.

"Finally getting away for that long overdue honeymoon?" Regine said, smiling.

Andy recovered. "Yes. With our crazy schedules it was impossible to do it before. We needed to get away from the media frenzy anyway."

"You picked a great spot at a great time of the year. The island is practically deserted."

"It's exactly what we were hoping for," he replied. He looked over at his wife. "Wouldn't you agree?"

"Ab-absolutely," Vanessa replied.

"Now that you're here, we'll be able to spend some time getting to know each other," Regine said. "That sounds like a terrific idea, right, babe?"

The other man replied in a neutral tone, "Sounds good, though we wouldn't want to monopolize all your time. They are on their honeymoon after all."

The implication in Bryce's tone rankled Andy, but he kept his tone neutral. "Appreciate your understanding, Bryce. And with that, we'll say good night. Enjoy your evening." He eased his arm around Vanessa's back and guided her towards the exit.

The other couple took their seats and waited until their waiter took their drink order before Regine uttered, "You son-of-a-bitch."

~ ~ ~

Despite the warm air blowing off the ocean, there was a definite chill surrounding Andy and Vanessa. Neither said a word as they proceeded to their cabin. Once they entered, Vanessa grabbed Andy's arm and said, "Please, Andy, let's talk."

"What's there to talk about?"

"I'm sorry. I didn't know they were coming here."

"They? Or her?"

"That's uncalled for!"

"Really? Tell me, sweetheart, who was the friend who told you about this lovely island paradise in the first place?" She turned away. "That's what I thought. You're a piece of work, you know that?"

"Andy, please."

"You wanted seclusion, now you have it. At least you had the decency to wait until we were out of town. I appreciate your discretion. Good night." He crossed the sitting area in a couple of strides and slammed the door to his bedroom.

Furious, she ran to his room and threw open the door. "You don't get to talk to me like that and expect me to lie down and take it! I didn't know either of them were coming; I certainly didn't invite them! Yes, I told Bryce I was leaving and where I was going and that I was going with you. I didn't expect that he'd follow me here and bring his wife along. I'm sure she was just as dismayed by seeing us here as you were.

"Just one more thing: do you really think that I'd disrespect you by throwing my relationship with Bryce in your face? That I'd bring you here just so I could sneak away and sleep with him? If I wanted to do that, I would have come here by myself. Nice to know you think so little of me." She left and slammed the door behind her. She crossed the room into her own bedroom, threw her clothes on the floor, and turned on the shower. As the water pounded her body, she began to cry, grateful the sound of the water masked her sobbing.

Andy sat on the floor outside Vanessa's room. He could hear her crying and his heart ached. Part of him still was angry, but part of him wanted to believe she was telling the truth. He got up and went to his room and knelt down by the bed. "Father," he pleaded, "help me."

CHAPTER EIGHTEEN

Company

Andy's restless night caused him to get up early. He felt bad about the way he left things with Vanessa but his pride refused to let him go to her and apologize. It made no sense to keep lying in bed since he wasn't sleeping. He got up and threw on a jersey and a pair of shorts and sandals. He was about to leave when he saw his Bible on the nightstand. He grabbed it and quietly went out the door.

The sun was barely in the sky as he walked along the deserted beachfront. With the exception of the ocean waves and the occasional bird noises, it was completely silent. It had been a long time since he'd enjoyed this type of quiet. He felt his spirit quieting down and readying for a time of worship and prayer. He lifted his hands and began praying, first to himself and then aloud. He recalled verse after verse of Scripture that declared God's goodness and mercy, and he thanked the Lord for all his blessings. He began praying for forgiveness for his attitude and his harsh treatment of his wife.

He also began praying for Vanessa in earnest, that she would be able to make wise decisions about her life and her relationships. At this point, he collapsed on the white sands. Confessing his confusion, he prayed, "Lord, You told me to enter into this marriage. You said to trust you. And I am. I didn't go into this expecting anything other than a way to save the mission. But being with Vanessa, spending time with her, I realize that all those feelings I had for her, the love I had for her, it's all coming back. I know now they never really went away. Yet, here we are, and her boyfriend's here. Sometimes I think she feels the same way. Sometimes I think she only considers this a business transaction. And it's driving me nuts! A little help here, God?"

He hung his head and waited. The only words that registered in his spirit were: *Trust Me.*

For how long?

Trust Me.

Andy rolled his eyes and shook his head. "I'll trust You, Lord." He smiled as the words to an old hymn popped into his head: *I will trust in the Lord, I will trust in the Lord, I will trust in the Lord until I die.*

"What's so funny?" Regine asked.

Andy looked up and saw her standing in front of him, grinning. She was wearing a sleeveless running tank and shorts. From the sweat dripping from her body, it was clear she had been running for a while. A thought crossed his mind: *Is this Your idea of a joke?* "Good morning, Regine."

"Morning. What's so funny?"

"What makes you think I'm laughing at anything?'

"When I ran up to you, you were smiling so something had to be funny."

"It's nothing. I was just meditating and an old hymn popped into my head, one I haven't heard in a long time." He stood up and brushed the sand off himself. "How are you this morning?"

"I'm good. I decided to take advantage of this beautiful morning to get a run in. It's so peaceful out here. Helps me clear my head. I didn't expect to run into you."

"Same here. Where's Bryce?"

"Sleeping in. Or checking his emails. Who knows? And where is your bride?"

"Sleeping in I'm sure. She's a morning person, but not quite this early."

"Oh. Say have you had breakfast yet?"

"Nope. I was waiting for Vanessa." They laughed as his stomach growled. "Guess that changes things."

"Would you like a little company?"

"What about Bryce?"

"He'll just have coffee in the cabin. I need to eat. Especially after my run."

"In that case, I wouldn't mind the company at all."

"Good. Let me shower and change and I'll meet you at the restaurant in ten minutes." She jogged off back towards her cabin. Andy smiled as he walked back to his own cabin to drop off his Bible. Vanessa was still asleep so he left her a note. "Couldn't sleep. Went up to the main house to get some breakfast. Sorry about last night. Let's talk later."

~ ~ ~

Over a hearty breakfast, Andy and Regine talked about themselves. She revealed that she once had aspirations of becoming a teacher. After completing her undergraduate studies, she taught for a year while enrolled in grad school, but never finished.

"What happened?" Andy asked.

"I met Bryce," she replied. "He was a star on the rise and he wanted me to be beside him. He told me if I would take care of him, he'd take care of me——and he has."

"Do you regret not following your heart?"

"Being a teacher? With what they make? No, I don't regret it at all. Okay, sometimes I do. There's a part of me that wants to give back to the community. So I do some charity work, participate in fundraisers, that sort of thing. We've been so blessed, it's only right that we pay it forward."

"And it doesn't hurt Bryce's status to have a gorgeous wife getting her photo taken on the social register."

She chuckled. "Exactly. You have a way of seeing straight to the heart of a matter. No B.S. I like that about you."

"Thanks. So, your charity work, that's how you met Vanessa?"

"Yes. I worked with her mother at a literacy event. I liked the work of the Carson Foundation and I wanted to be a part of it. I twisted Bryce's arm to get his firm to be a major donor to the foundation. It's been mutually beneficial for everyone."

"Including you?"

She chuckled again. "There you go again. Straight shootin' preacher Andy."

"I didn't mean to imply..."

"Yes, you did." She stopped smiling and began picking at the food remnants on her plate. "Tell me something, Andy, straight up. Why did you marry Vanessa?"

"Excuse me?"

"I read the interview you two did. I just didn't buy it. Vanessa is not exactly the low-key type and if she wanted to be married, it would have been the event of the season, even if it was at the last minute. People would have dropped everything to see Vanessa Carson get married. You just came out of nowhere and convinced her to elope. I don't buy it."

"You don't believe that love can happen instantly?"

"Sure. I don't believe weddings happen instantly."

"We both knew what we wanted and with her mother's recent passing, Vanessa didn't want to wait. I didn't need a big wedding. We just decided to keep it small and intimate. In my experience, I think too many couples spend too much time planning for a wedding and not enough time preparing for a marriage." He took a sip of his coffee. "Your turn? Why did you marry Bryce?"

"Because I loved him."

"Loved, past tense?"

"It was a slip of the tongue." She pointed her fork at him. "Don't go reading anything into that."

"If you say so."

"I say so. Look, I'm not stupid. I've known for a long time about Bryce and Vanessa. But after I found out that she got married, I thought there was a chance for us to start over. And for a while, things were going really well between us. When he said he wanted to get away for a vacation, I thought it was going to be a second honeymoon. I had no idea that the two of you were going to be here."

"The feeling was mutual. So how does it make you feel?"

"Like a fool. This is not the way I envisioned my marriage playing out. But I've learned to live with it."

"Have you? Is this what you really want?"

"What I really want is to not talk about this anymore. What I want is to enjoy myself. What are your plans for today?"

He shrugged. "We hadn't really planned anything. I'm open. I heard there was some deep sea fishing going on."

"You're into deep sea fishing?"

"I've never tried it, but I've always wanted to."

"Want some company?"

"Sure. What about Bryce?"

"What about him? He hates fishing."

"You don't mind if I ask Vanessa to join us, do you?"

"Why not? Maybe she'll fall off the boat." She laughed, but Andy wondered if she wasn't partly serious.

"Good. I'll see if she wants to come along. I'll check the charter schedule and give you a call." He stood. "Thank you for breakfast. I really enjoyed talking with you."

"Me too. I'll see you later." She watched him leave, a smile spreading across her face. Maybe this will turn out better than I thought.

CHAPTER NINETEEN

Please

Andy entered the villa and saw Vanessa exiting her bedroom, tying a scarf around her hair. "You're just going out?"

"Yes. I was heading up to the lodge for breakfast." She brushed past him but he grabbed her by the wrist.

"I'm sorry about last night. My words were harsh and cruel. I shouldn't have accused you of playing me. That wasn't fair. I hope you'll forgive me."

She smiled. "I'm sorry too. I really didn't expect to run into Bryce and Regine here. I just wanted us to get away and relax for a while. Forgive me?"

"Forgiven."

"Care to join me for breakfast?"

"I already ate. I got up early to pray and then I got hungry." He picked up the note he left for her on the table. "I didn't know how long you were planning to sleep in and I didn't want to disturb you."

"Oh."

"But if you don't mind, allow me to walk with you to the lodge. I wanted to check on the deep-sea charters I read about. Would you like to join me?"

She shook her head. "I'll pass." At his disappointed expression, she added, "I'm not much of a fisherman. I was thinking of just unwinding on the beach with a good book. But you go on ahead. I'll meet you for dinner this evening."

"Sounds like a plan." He extended his arm and she took it and they walked along the beach. He ignored his conscience poking at him to tell her about Regine. *It's irrelevant. Why stir up trouble when we've just made up?*

~ ~ ~

The sun was a little brighter than Vanessa anticipated so she decided to relax on the villa's patio. Stretching out on the chaise lounge with a pitcher of iced tea at her side, she opened up her novel and began reading. An hour later, she looked up as a shadow fell across the tiles. "Hello, Bryce."

"Vanessa. Mind if I join you?" She gestured towards one of the chairs and he took a seat. "Is it good?"

"Is what good?"

"The book."

"Yeah, it's pretty good. It's the author's first book but it's not bad at all." She closed it and poured herself a glass of tea. She offered one to him, but he declined. Taking a sip, she said, "I'm surprised to see you here."

"Where? Your patio?"

"No, I mean here at the resort. When I told you I was going away, I didn't expect you to follow me and I certainly didn't expect you to bring your wife."

"I didn't intend on bringing her. She saw a note I'd written about this place and assumed I was planning a getaway for the two of us. I couldn't very well tell her what I was really planning."

"And what exactly were you planning?"

He reached over and stroked her calf. "To spend some time with you. Alone."

"With Andy here."

"Why would that be a problem? You said the two of you had an understanding."

"We do. That doesn't mean I'd bring him down here and disrespect him by going off with another man."

"I'm not just another man, V."

"I know." She pulled her legs away from his touch. "Even so, this was supposed to be a vacation for the two of us. You know that."

"I do. And now that we're alone, we can spend some special time with each other."

She frowned. "Where's your wife?"

"Gone fishing. With your husband." When she squirmed, he grinned. "I take it he didn't mention that little fact to you before he left."

"It's no big deal. I'm sure they'll have some fun, as friends."

"Maybe we could have some fun too, as friends."

"I told you, I'm not disrespecting Andy."

"Like he disrespected you?" He moved over and sat on the edge of the lounger. "If he's this honorable minister, why didn't he tell you he was going fishing with Regine?" He took her hand in his, rubbing the back of it with his thumb. "He didn't say anything because he didn't want you to know."

"Know what?"

"That he has feelings for her. She mentioned that they had breakfast together and a long talk. They seem to be getting close."

"That doesn't bother you?"

He shook his head as he eased closer to her. "The way I see it, if they can be friends, it'll make things easier between us." He reached up and stroked her cheek. "I don't want Regine to be lonely. If she can find some companionship with Andy, that works for both of us." He leaned in and gently kissed the base of her neck. "I can't hide how I feel about you much longer, Vanessa. I want you." He continued kissing her neck until she moaned. "You want this as badly as I do, don't you?" His other hand moved and began stroking the inside of her thigh. She moaned again and he whispered, "Please baby, please. Don't say no."

"Oh God," she whispered. She turned her head to capture his lips in a passionate kiss. A sudden gust of wind blew across the patio, causing her to shiver. She pulled back. "No. I can't do this, Bryce. I'm sorry."

"Vanessa..."

"No, Bryce. I promised Andy that I would honor my vows. As bad as I want you——and I do want you——I can't take chances. If Andy and I don't finish out this year, I could lose everything. I'm sorry." She got up from the chaise and ran inside the villa, closing the patio doors behind her.

He swore, got up and headed in the direction of his own villa.

~ ~ ~

A few hours later, Andy returned to the villa to find his wife sitting casually in the living area sipping a drink. "Hey, Vanessa."

"Hey yourself. How was fishing?"

"It was great. I've always wanted to go deep-sea fishing. It looked like so much fun. But I never realized how hard it really is!" He rubbed his shoulder. "I thought I was in shape, but pulling one of those marlins out was something else!"

"You caught something?"

"Oh yeah. Just one. But it was huge! I guess the rule is if you catch it, you give it up to the local market, which turns it over to the chefs here. We may be eating my catch of the day for dinner tonight."

"Sounds good."

He peered at her face. "You okay?"

"I'm fine."

"You sure?"

"Yes, I'm sure." She patted the seat next to her and he flopped down on the loveseat. "Want something to drink?"

"Is there beer in there?"

"Yes. It's a local brew but I'm told it's pretty good." She got up and went to the refrigerator and pulled out a bottle. She opened it and poured the liquid into a glass. She went back and handed it to him, taking a sip along the way. "It is pretty good."

"I'll be the judge." He took the glass and drank. "You're right, it is pretty good. Different, but good." He stretched a bit, then moaned. "I'm gonna be sore tonight."

"Would you like a massage?"

He grinned. "Are you offering?"

She slapped his arm. "Not a chance. But I can call and arrange for a masseuse to come over."

"That would be great. As long as you're sticking around. I don't want some strange woman trying to get her freak on with me."

She laughed. "For a preacher, you've got a sick sense of humor."

"It's the world I live in."

"Yeah, right." She picked up the phone and made the arrangements. "Speaking of getting your freak on, can I ask you something?"

"Shoot."

"Why didn't you tell me you were going with Regine?"

"Who told you that?"

"Bryce."

"What was he doing here?"

She held up her hands. "Hang on, preacher man. Don't flip this back on me. We talked, that's all." *That's all you need to know.* "He told me that the two of you went fishing and you had breakfast together. All I want to know is why you didn't mention it to me."

He sighed. "I suppose I should have. But after our fight last night, I didn't want to stir the pot. I didn't know how you'd react to me having breakfast with Bryce's wife."

"It wouldn't have made me any difference."

"Really."

"Yes, really." She saw the look of disbelief on his face. "Okay, it would have made a difference."

"Why?"

"Because Regine can be very manipulative. I just didn't want you getting caught up in something that you couldn't handle."

"Like you and Bryce."

She nodded. "Touché. I admit this whole situation is complicated, for more than one reason. But if Regine were to find out about me and Bryce——"

"She already knows."

"What?"

"Before you accuse me, I didn't tell her anything. She figured it out a long time ago. Bryce doesn't think she knows, but she does. Still, she's not ready to give up on her marriage. She was hoping this trip was a chance for a new start between them. You can imagine her surprise and disappointment when she saw us here."

Remembering her earlier dalliance with Bryce, Vanessa turned away. "I told him it was a mistake coming here." She turned back to face him. "I know what Bryce and I have done is wrong. I never wanted to hurt her. You have to believe me."

"I believe you never wanted to hurt anyone. But the fact is, you did. And if you still continue your relationship with him, you continue to hurt her and yourself. I know you can't always help who you fall in love with. But you can make the choice to do the right thing. Whether you do or not is up to you." He planted a kiss on her forehead and stood. "Let me know when the masseuse gets her. I'm gonna go shower."

As she watched him walk away, she sighed. *I guess you really can't help who you fall in love with.*

CHAPTER TWENTY

Peace

The next morning, Andy decided the only way to make things work with Vanessa was to include her completely in his life. That meant morning devotion. He knew she was a late riser, so he decided to have breakfast brought in to their villa. By the time she arose, showered, and dressed, Andy was sitting at the table waiting for her. "Good morning," he said. He stood and poured her a cup of coffee, which she took, gratefully.

"What's all this?"

"I realized I handled things badly yesterday. This was supposed to be our so-called honeymoon, or at the very least, a vacation. I should have made it a priority to spend time with you. I didn't and I'm sorry. Call this a peace offering; a reset, if you will. I hope you'll forgive me and allow me a chance to make it up to you."

She sipped her coffee, then smiled. "I think I should be the one to apologize. This whole thing was my idea. I didn't have a right to drag you into my mess, then expect you to play by my rules."

"Let's just say we're even and wipe the slate clean." He walked around the table and pulled out a chair for her.

"Mmmm...what's on the menu?"

"Let's see," he said, pulling the silver tops off the platters. "Fresh fruit, croissants with butter, honey and orange glaze, fresh salmon, poached eggs, coffee, orange juice, and," he went and grabbed a high hat and set it in front of her, "champagne."

"I see. What's the champagne for?"

"Depends. We can celebrate our marriage, toast our deal, or just have a mimosa or two."

"I like the way you ask for forgiveness." She picked up her flute and waited as he filled the glass halfway with orange juice and half with champagne. He did the same to his glass, then lifted it in a toast. "To new beginnings," she said.

"To happy endings," he replied.

~ ~ ~

After breakfast, Andy invited Vanessa to join him in morning devotion. She frowned at first, but agreed after he promised that it wouldn't be a lecture about her relationship with Bryce. "I was thinking about us and a Scripture came to mind, Jeremiah 29:11." He handed her his Bible. "Read it."

She took the Bible. "For I know the thoughts that I think toward you, saith Jehovah, thoughts of peace, and not of evil, to give you hope in your latter end." She looked up at him.

"What does that mean to you?"

She sat back on the couch and looked up. "I guess I'd have to say it means that God wants good things for us and He knows what those things are. What do you think it means?"

"I believe it means that God has a divine plan for each of our lives. Because we are His children, He wants us to benefit from the goodness and blessings that He has in store for us. It's up to us to trust in Him and allow Him to lead us."

"But how can you be sure of what His plan is? I mean, when I think of all the twists my life has taken, how do I know what He's doing?"

"Because the Bible reassures us in Psalms 139, verse 16." He took the Bible and quickly flipped to a highlighted passage. "Thine eyes did see mine unformed substance; And in thy book they were all written, Even the days that were ordained for me, when as yet there was none of them." He turned to another scripture. "Isaiah 55:6 and 7 says, 'For my thoughts are not your thoughts, neither are your ways my ways, saith Jehovah. For as the heavens are higher than the earth, so are my ways higher than your ways, and my thoughts than your thoughts.' He knew before we were born the path and direction our lives would take."

"And He knew how badly we would screw them up?"

Andy laughed. "Yeah, I guess He did."

Vanessa leaned back and smirked. "Okay, Mr. Bible-Answer-Man, riddle me this: if He knows everything about us and how we would screw up our lives, how do you explain us?"

"Us?"

"Yes, us. You once told me that God had designed for us to be together. Yet, we broke up —"

"You broke up with me."

"Whatever. The point is, we weren't together. And now we are, although not necessarily for the same reasons we once were."

He leaned back. It was his turn to smirk. "Exactly. We are together."

"We have an arrangement. A business deal. We didn't marry for love; we married for money. And once the terms of our deal have been fulfilled, then what?"

The smirk vanished from his face. He shrugged. "I don't know."

She turned away for a moment. "What if it isn't his will? What if his will is for us to be with other people?"

He sighed. He knew she was thinking about Bryce. If he were completely honest with himself, he knew that Regine was in the back of his mind. "I know what the Bible says about adultery. You know it as well. Can God bless a relationship that is borne out of deception, out of the will of God? He could. Will he? That's not for me to say."

He took her hand in his, and with his other, he turned her face back to him. "What I do know is that I prayed for a way to save the mission. He answered that prayer through you. I don't believe it was a coincidence. I believe it was divine providence. And I am grateful that he brought you back into my life, in spite of the circumstances. I don't know what the future holds for us. I can only deal with now. And for now, I have a beautiful lady as my friend and as my wife. I promise to do my best to make you happy."

Vanessa nodded. "For what it's worth, I'm glad to have you back in my life, too. And I promise to do my best to keep your life as uncomplicated as possible."

He chuckled. "Vanessa, with you, nothing is ever uncomplicated."

"What's that supposed to mean?"

He kissed her on the cheek and stood up. "It means that I want to go swimming in that beautiful ocean outside."

CHAPTER TWENTY-ONE

Challenge

It took everything within Vanessa to control the desires stirring inside her as Andy emerged from the ocean. The bright morning sun caused the water dripping down his body to glisten, giving him an almost otherworldly glow about him. When he reached up to brush the water from his eyes, she could see every cut in his musculature. She knew he was fit; she had no idea just how toned his physique really was.

As he jogged towards her, she put on her large sunglasses to mask the desire in her eyes. "Did you have a nice swim?"

"Whew!" He collapsed on the towel next to her. "I have had some great workouts in the pool, but it's nothing like swimming in the ocean. Even though the current isn't that strong, swimming against the waves really did me in!"

"You look like you're up for the challenge."

He grinned, then flexed. "Well, you know, what can I say?"

She groaned. "Please. You've been watching TV Land again, haven't you?"

"I can't help it." He rolled over to face her. "Wouldn't you like to take a dip?"

She shook her head. "No, I'm fine right where I am."

"Aw, come on. It's beautiful. The sun is shining, the water is clean, clear, and oh, so crystal blue. Plus it's extremely warm."

"No thanks."

"I heard the water of the ocean can be very invigorating. It's supposed to help you loosen your inhibitions."

She peered over the top of her sunglasses. "Where did you hear that?"

"I don't know, some show. But it's true."

"I doubt it. Plus, I don't want to mess up my hair."

"No one around here will care if your hair is messed up. Plus, I happen to know you brought enough hair products to start a beauty supply store on the island." He chuckled. "Listen, we're on vacation, on our honeymoon, no less. Live a little."

"No."

"Please?"

"No!"

"Pretty please?"

"I hate to see a grown man beg."

"Fine." He rolled over and popped up on his knees. "I'm sorry it had to come to this, but you leave me no choice." He leaned over and scooped her up in his arms.

"Andy! Put me down."

"Nope. Sorry." He awkwardly stood, finding his footing on the sand. As she began kicking and beating on his back, he grinned and walked straight to the water.

"Put me down!"

He hummed, "Take Me to the Water," taking great strides into the ocean. The minute he finished the phrase, "to be baptized", he tossed Vanessa into the ocean. He threw his head back and laughed heartily enjoying the sight of his wife splashing around the water, trying to get her bearing. He was so distracted with laughter that he didn't see her flip over and under and move toward him. His laughter turned into a scream as she grabbed his legs and pulled them from under him. When he emerged, he looked up and saw a dripping Vanessa smirking at him.

"When you least expect it," she said, "expect it."

He grinned as she stomped out of the water. He knew she was mad, but he also knew she'd get over it. And that she gave as good as she got.

~ ~ ~

After their playtime in the ocean, the couple decided to take a ride on the available jet skis. After a brief lesson, Vanessa and Andy were racing off into the ocean. About a mile out, Vanessa idled her jet ski and waited as Andy rode up beside her. "What's up?" he asked.

"How about a little wager?"

"What kind of wager?"

"We race down to the end of the cabanas and back again."

"What are the stakes?"

"Loser has to do whatever the winner says for the next 24 hours."

He raised his eyebrows. "Really? What's off limits?"

She arched one of her own. "Nothing." The smile she gave him sent shivers down his spine.

Never one to back down from a challenge, he replied, "You're on. Countdown from 3-2-1-GO!"

The two jet skis raced across the ocean's waves. They bobbed and jumped as each tried to cross in front of the other. When they reached their endpoint, they circled around each other trying to stay ahead of the other. They were just about even when Vanessa suddenly crossed in front of Andy's jet ski. The wake she created caught Andy off guard; he tried to jump but was off balance and tumbled into the water. As he rose to the surface and swam back to his overturned vehicle, he heard Vanessa laughing and cheering in the distance. I should have seen that coming.

Just as he climbed on board, she came roaring back. "You okay?"

"I'm fine."

"I suppose you think I cheated."

"Nope. I deserved that."

"I still win."

"I know. I'll honor the bet."

"Good. We'll be spending the rest of the day in our cabin."

He felt his skin grow warm. It took a minute for him to find his voice. "Doing what, exactly?"

She leaned over close and said, "Whatever I want."

CHAPTER TWENTY-TWO

Whatever

"Whatever" turned out to be an afternoon of pampering. Vanessa arranged for in-room his and her massages, manicures, and pedicures. Andy started to object, but she reminded him of the bet. The manicurist laughed at Andy's pinched expression, then reassured him that there would be no polish used on either his hands or feet. The foot and hand rubs were soothing and by the time the masseuses arrived for the massage, Andy was warmed up.

Andy was wearing a pair of boxer briefs and stretched out across his table. The masseuse draped a sheet over his bottom. He turned to see Vanessa entering wearing one of the resort's plush robes. "I thought you were getting a massage," he said.

"I am," she replied. "It's a full body massage." Her masseuse held up a sheet to cover her lower half, then Vanessa turned and dropped the robe. Andy quickly turned away, glad he was lying face down and covered. He heard her chuckling as she adjusted herself on the table. *I don't see why she thinks this is funny. If she only knew...*

"You are very tense, mister," his masseuse was saying. "Just relax."

He grimaced as the woman began kneading his back and shoulder muscles. He turned his head and noticed Vanessa laying on her front, her head facing him. Her eyes were closed and she had a soft smile on her face. It was clear she had no problem relaxing. He couldn't help but notice the suppleness of her skin, the way her body curved and arched in all the right places. She began to moan softly as the masseuse worked his magic over her body.

"You're getting all tense again, mister."

You have no idea. He turned his head away from her and closed his eyes. It would be so easy to send these people away and just.... *No, that's not happening. We have a deal. No strings. No complications. Help me, Lord.* The tune of an old hymn came to mind, and he let the melody flow through him, gradually taking his mind off of his current situation.

He felt a tap on his shoulder. "Huh?" He groggily turned over to see Vanessa standing before him clad in her bathrobe.

"You must have really enjoyed the massage. You were knocked out."

"Really?" He yawned. "How long have I been out?"

"I don't know. I heard you humming, then nothing. The masseuse has been gone for about thirty minutes."

"Wow." He sat up, stretching out his body. He was suddenly aware of how he was dressed and grabbed the sheet and wrapped it around himself. "I haven't felt this good in a long time."

"I'm glad you enjoyed it."

"I did. Best bet I ever lost."

"Good. We should get dressed for dinner." She turned and sauntered out the room and into her bedroom. After she closed the door, he stood. "I think I need to shower first," he muttered.

CHAPTER TWENTY-THREE

Running

Thirty minutes later, Andy emerged from his room, showered and dressed for dinner. "Vanessa?" There was no response. He checked through the villa; she was nowhere to be found. He stepped out on the patio and glanced around. He saw her standing at the water's edge a few yards away.

As he walked toward her, he saw her arms wrapped around herself. She was staring out at the horizon. She didn't seem to hear him walking towards her. Rather than startling her, he said softly, "Vanessa?"

She turned to him then back again. "Hey."

"Hey yourself." He waited a few minutes staring out across the water. "This is such a beautiful place." She nodded but otherwise remained silent. He heard her sniff, so he looked at her and saw tears streaming down

175

her face. He moved until he was behind her, then wrapped his arms around her. He felt her fingers wrap around his forearms, and he nestled his head on her shoulder so that his cheek was next to hers.

"I miss my mom," she whispered. Within seconds, her whole body was convulsing with sobs. He turned her around in his arms until her head was buried in his chest. He drew her close, wrapping her tighter in his arms, supporting her as her legs would no longer support her weight. He let her cry, whispering words of comfort to her, sending up prayers for her.

As her sobs subsided, she regained her strength and stood up. "I'm sorry," she whispered.

"Don't apologize. But I think I may need to change my shirt," he said, smiling.

She chuckled. "Yeah, I think you might." She looked up at him, eyes swollen from her tears. "I'm pretty sure I need to fix my makeup. I'm a mess."

"You're fine." He wrapped his arm around her shoulders and they walked back towards their villa. Once there, they both disappeared into their respective rooms. Within five minutes, they were both back in the living room, Andy in a fresh shirt, and Vanessa with touched up makeup. She smiled at Andy. "Sorry about your shirt."

"It's fine. I'm more concerned about you."

She shrugged. "I don't know what came over me out there. I was waiting for you to come out. I was standing on the beach, looking at the sunset, and I thought about the last time I was here. I started thinking about my mother and it just hit me."

"It's no wonder. You've had to deal with your mother's illness and managing the foundation for a year, then her death. You barely had time to come to terms with that, when you were hit with the terms of her will, our marriage, and all the chaos that has come as a result of it." He took her hands in his. "You've never really had all that much time to grieve."

"I thought I was over it."

"You're never over losing a parent. You get through it."

"Is that how you dealt with losing your father?"

"I guess so. I was only seven when he died, so it was a bit different for me. I remember crying a lot. And my mom couldn't talk about him for a long time without crying. But as the years went on, we've been able to talk about him and share memories. I feel like I know him a lot better even though he wasn't with me. The good thing is that you have lots of memories of your mom and dad. And one day, you'll be able to think about them without crying."

"And until then?"

"I've got lots of shirts." That elicited a laugh. Andy laughed with her. "Let's go to dinner."

~ ~ ~

There were several new couples at the restaurant. Andy and Vanessa opted for a window seat near the corner of the restaurant. As soon as they were seated, Bryce and Regine walked over. "Well, well, well," Regine said, "small world. Mind if we join you?"

Before Vanessa could object, Andy stood. "Of course. If that's fine with you, Bryce."

The other man shrugged, then took a seat. Regine cleared her throat.

"What?" Bryce responded.

Regine nodded her head at the empty chair. He rolled his eyes, stood, and pulled out the chair, and then sat back down. The waiter came over and took their drink orders. The couples sat in silence for a while, until Andy spoke up. "So, how did the two of you meet?"

Regine smiled. "At school. I was coordinating Career Day. I wanted to bring in professionals——especially professional black men——to expose my kids to different careers other than rapper, basketball player, or singer. I read Bryce's profile in Ebony and on a whim, I looked him up, then contacted him. I charmed him into coming. It was definitely interest at first sight."

Bryce nodded. "I thought she was too cute to be a teacher. I never had teachers that looked like her."

Andy nodded. "Me either."

"But she was so good with the kids; it was amazing to watch."

"So why did you stop teaching?"

"I wanted to support my husband. And I felt the best way was for me to be at home. I wanted to make sure that he could come home to a loving and nurturing environment, free from the stresses of the office. I hosted parties for the office, set up client dinners, whatever it took for him to become a success. It didn't matter to me that I had given up my career. His success was——is——my success." She smiled in her husband's face, as he took a sip of his drink.

The waiter came and took their dinner orders and refreshed their drinks. "So, Andy and Vanessa. Tell us how you met."

"You already know our story," Vanessa replied.

"Not that story. I want to know how you met the first time. Clearly, you had a thing, since you two reconnected so easily."

"I... well..." She turned away.

Andy reached under the table and squeezed her hand. "A couple of students on campus were killed in a hit and run accident. I was a student counselor. Vanessa came to me asking for prayer. We talked and before long, we developed feelings for each other."

"Andy was amazing," Vanessa said. "He helped me come to terms with my friends' deaths. And he just understood me. He listened when I talked, even when I didn't always make sense. Over time, I found we had a lot of things in common."

"I find that hard to believe," Bryce snorted.

Vanessa ignored him. She stared at Andy. "He had the kindest heart, the gentlest spirit. I think that's what attracted me the most. Plus, he has a wicked sense of humor."

"I give as good as I get," Andy said, grinning.

"So why did you break up?" Regine asked.

The other couple stared at each other. Andy spoke first. "Vanessa wasn't ready for the kind of commitment I wanted. To be fair, she was still in school and I was on my way to grad school and ministry work."

"You mean, she wasn't ready to be a preacher's wife," Bryce said, smirking. "Vanessa wanted something more from life."

"And what Vanessa wants, Vanessa gets," Regine said, her voice laced with sarcasm.

Vanessa dropped Andy's hand then stood. "Andy, we should go pack."

"What?"

"You're leaving? What about dinner? We were having such a pleasant time," Regine said.

"I thought you were staying for the week," Bryce added.

"No, our plans have changed. We're leaving tomorrow."

"We are?" Andy asked.

"Yes. We've been gone long enough as it is, and you yourself said you couldn't afford to be away from your work for more than a couple of days."

"I did say that, but——"

"Please, Andy." Her voice began to crack. "We need to go now." She turned to the other couple. "I'm sorry about everything. I hope you enjoy the rest of your stay." She excused herself from the table just as the waiter appeared with their plates.

"You're welcome to stay, Andy," Regine purred.

"I don't think so." Andy stood and spoke to the waiter, who removed both his and Vanessa's plates from the table. "Perhaps we'll see each other again stateside. Have a good evening, Bryce, Regine."

Bryce stared at his wife. "What's gotten into you?"

"Me? I was just trying to make friendly conversation. Can I help it if girlfriend is so sensitive?" She began to dig into her plate. "Mmmm...this food is delicious! You should try some of it."

He pushed his plate back. "I'm not hungry."

~ ~ ~

By the time Andy reached his villa, Vanessa was on the phone. Her suitcases were already near the door. "Yes, that's right," she was saying. "I'd like a 10:00 a.m. departure. If there are any problems, please let me know immediately. Thank you."

"What's going on?"

"We're leaving."

"So you said. Why?"

"I can't be here with...them."

"So you're running away?"

"I'm not running away. I'm going home. You're welcome to stay if you wish. The room is paid up until the end of the week and I can arrange for your transportation home."

"I'm not staying here without you. But you shouldn't leave either."

"Why not? It can't be pleasant for you to keep running into them on this tiny island."

"No, it's not pleasant. But I can handle it."

"I can't."

"So you just pack up and leave."

"Yes!"

He shook his head. "That's so typical of you, Vanessa. When things get complicated or messy, you just pack your bags and run away. Sooner or later, you're going to have to grow up and face your issues. If you're gonna run away every time life gets hard, you'll be running for the rest of your life." He headed into his room.

"Where are you going?"

"To pack. Wouldn't look good for newlyweds to come back home on separate flights."

CHAPTER TWENTY-FOUR

Complications

When they arrived home, they were greeted by Ella
——who had taken Vanessa up on her offer to move in
temporarily——and Phoebe. They were both were
delighted to see the couple getting along so well.

"The islands agree with you," Ella said, as they
settled down for a late evening snack.

"This place was beautiful," Andy declared. "I've
never seen sand so pure and white. And the ocean?
Crystal blue water as far as the eye could see. It's a far
cry from Lake Michigan. We'll have to take you there
next time, Mom. You'll love it."

"Next time?" Ella smiled, winking at Phoebe, who
had a small smile of her own.

"What's going on?" Vanessa asked, looking first at
her mother-in-law then back to her great-aunt. "What

have the two of you been cooking up while we've been gone?"

"Nothing at all, dear," Phoebe replied. "Ella simply remarked that such a secluded and romantic location could lead to something more."

"Something more?"

"Yes. A more permanent arrangement. You definitely seem closer than you were before you left."

Andy squirmed in his seat but said nothing. He looked to his wife for a response.

"You're right, Aunt Phoebe," she said. "Andy and I did spend a lot of time together. And we did get closer——as friends."

"Is that all?" Ella asked.

"Yes." She looked at her husband, but turned away from the pain lining his face.

Andy jumped up. "I'm going to make a sandwich. Does anyone want anything from the kitchen?" He barely waited for a reply before turning and heading for the kitchen.

~ ~ ~

Ella saw her son staring into the darkness as he leaned on the doorjamb by the patio doors. The tension in his lanky frame was evident by the visible veins lining the back of his neck. She knew better than to ask him anything. Instead, she grabbed a loaf of bread off the counter and put four slices into the toaster. While waiting for them, she pulled out two small plates and grabbed the peanut butter and jelly from the refrigerator. The toaster popped and she made two sandwiches, cut them in half and laid them on the plates. Then she poured two glasses of milk and sat down at the counter. She nibbled on her sandwich and waited.

Almost like clockwork, Andy came and sat next to her. He absently began chewing on his sandwich. After taking a drink, he said, "I think this was a mistake."

"The sandwich?"

"The marriage."

"Why?"

He shrugged. "I didn't count on things getting so complicated." He told her the situation with Vanessa, Bryce, and Regine, including the events that took place during the trip. "I didn't expect to be involved in so much drama. This was supposed to be a simple arrangement: get married, get the money, and get out. It's what we both agreed to."

"So what's changed?"

"I don't know."

"I think you do. Do you love Vanessa?"

"Of course I do, Mom. She's my friend."

"Are you in love with her?"

"What? Mom, that's a dumb question."

"Then answer it."

"It's not that simple."

"Yes, it is." Her tone softened as she laid a hand on his cheek. "Are you in love with Vanessa?"

He sighed. "I think I am."

"Then tell her."

"I can't."

"Why not?"

"Haven't you been listening? She's not in love with me. She's in love with Bryce."

"Did she tell you that?"

"Yes."

"Really?"

"Okay, not in so many words. But you heard what she said out there. The only thing between us is friendship."

Ella sighed. *Young people made things so difficult.* "Did it ever occur to you that she said what she thought you wanted to hear? Perhaps she's afraid of getting her heart broken if she thinks you don't feel the same way." She leaned over, kissed him on the head then stood. "I'm heading up to bed. Think about what I said."

~ ~ ~

"Friends. Really."

"Don't start, Aunt Phoebe."

"The young man that stormed out of here doesn't think of you as a friend." Taking a sip of her tea, she added, "And I suspect that you don't feel that way either."

"That's not true," Vanessa replied, turning her face to avoid her aunt's disapproving gaze.

Phoebe continued sipping her tea. "Your father was a terrible poker player."

"What?"

"Yes, you see he was never very good at lying or hiding his feelings. Whenever he lied or had some unpleasant news to share, he would turn his head and stare off into space. No matter how hard I tried, I couldn't shake him from it. You seem to have inherited the same trait."

She sat her cup down and folded her hands. "There's nothing wrong if you're developing feelings for Andy. He is, after all, your husband. And he was your first love. It's perfectly natural."

Vanessa shook her head. "There can never be anything more than friendship between us, Aunt Phoebe."

"And why not?"

"Because!" She stood and started pacing. "Because I hurt him too bad before. Because we live in two different worlds. Because he's an honorable man and he understands the terms of our agreement and he'll abide by them."

"What if he wants to change the terms?"

"Meaning what?"

"Meaning what if he feels differently? What if he's in love with you and wants to stay married?"

"Aunt Phoebe! You're the last person I'd expect to encourage me to stay married to a minister, especially one that runs a shelter for runaway and pregnant teens."

"Granted, he wouldn't have been my first choice for you. But Andy seems like a good man. And he seems to make you happy. Does he?"

Vanessa dropped down to the ottoman in front of her aunt's chair. "He does. He always has."

"Then you have your answer."

"It's not that simple. There are... complications."

"Complications?"

Vanessa sighed. Phoebe knew nothing of her relationship with Bryce. "Yes. It's late and I really don't want to get into this tonight." She leaned over and kissed her aunt's cheek. "I love you, Aunt Phoebe. Good night."

"Good night, dear one." She smiled to herself as she picked up her teacup. *Complications indeed. We are most certainly going to get into it.*

CHAPTER TWENTY-FIVE

Stand

Andy was glad when Monday morning rolled around. He missed his "kids" terribly and was anxious to catch up with Kendra. Plus, if he admitted it to himself, it was good to get back into his routine, to avoid having to deal with his confusing feelings and his mother's nagging questions.

Speaking of his mother, he realized he missed having Ella around. He tried to convince her to stay, but she insisted on moving back to her own house, especially since it appeared that the media had moved on to another target. Vanessa also tried to convince her mother-in-law to stay, suggesting that she and Phoebe could keep each other company. Ella wouldn't budge.

As soon as he pulled up in front of the building, Kendra greeted him at the door, holding a stack of messages. "You've got a boatload of emails to return and the city inspector is supposed to be coming through again. We had 25 new intakes and 14 who left. I've had to break up 12 fights, I nearly cussed out one of the board members, you don't pay me nearly enough, and I really need a vacation."

"Good to see you, too," he replied, taking the messages out of her hands. "Which one?"

"Which one what?"

"Which board member did you nearly cuss out?"

"That Evelyn Freeman. She's such a busybody. She came in here, calling herself doing her 'Christian duty' and overseeing the place in your absence. Like I don't know how to do my job! Almost gave her a Holy Ghost pimp slap upside her head, in Jesus' name."

Andy couldn't help but laugh. Despite her blustering, he knew Kendra would never do anything disrespectful to a church mother. There was too much of her home training still in her. "I appreciate your restraint. And, you're right; I don't pay you enough. And I know you need a vacation. Now that we can afford to hire an intern, as soon as we can get one in and you can train him or her, you can take some time off."

"Hallelujah!" She started dancing right in front of his desk.

"Contact the local colleges and get a notice out. You prescreen the applicants and narrow it down to a few good ones. We'll get somebody in here as soon as possible."

She stopped dancing. "Great. More work for me." She flopped down in the chair.

"I know you're tired, Kendra. Look, now that I'm back, why don't you catch me up on things. If you want to take a couple of days later this week, you can do it."

She sat up straight. "You're serious? I'm not getting punked, am I?"

"No. This place couldn't make it without you and I know you've been running on fumes. Take a few days and recharge your batteries. Go to that place you're always talking about and pamper yourself. My treat."

"For real? You'd pay for my day at the Red Door Spa downtown?"

"Yeah, that's the one. Make an appointment for whatever you want. I'll take care of the bill."

She jumped up, shouted, and hugged Andy in such dizzying fashion he nearly fell over his chair. "You're the best!" She kissed his cheek. "Thank you! Thank you!" She released him then twirled around the office. "I'm getting the works! Massage, mani, pedi, facial, body scrub——"

"Whoa! TMI! Just get whatever you want and I've got you covered. I know you could probably use more time, but it'll have to wait until we can get an intern to cover for you."

"That's no problem! I'm just so grateful for what I can get."

"Good. Now catch me up."

~ ~ ~

Andy stretched in his chair. He'd been reviewing reports all morning and hadn't realized he'd been sitting in the same position for hours. "Oww," he called out, stretching his neck muscles. Maybe he needed to set up an appointment for a massage as well.

"You look like you could use a good massage."

He glanced up and saw Regine standing in the doorway. "Hey. You read my mind. What brings you by?"

"Just wanted to say hi. I was in the neighborhood."

"You were not."

"Okay, I wasn't. But I did want to stop by and say hello. It's not like I had anything else to do. I thought I might tempt you into heading out to lunch with me." When he inadvertently groaned, she crossed over and stood behind his chair. "Looks like lunch isn't what you really need." She began massaging his neck and shoulders, first gently then applying more pressure where needed.

Andy sighed. Regine's ministrations were just what he needed. He closed his eyes and let her knead his aching shoulders and neck into submission.

"Feel better?"

"Mmmm. Yeah. That's the ticket."

She continued the massage before asking, "We're friends, right?"

"Mm-hmmm."

"Good. I was just checking."

"Why'd you ask?"

"Because after our fishing adventure, you just up and disappeared. You and Vanessa snuck out of there so fast, I didn't even get a chance to say goodbye. And since you've been home, you've been in hiding. I just thought I did something wrong."

The conversation he had with his mother flashed through his mind. He reached up and took her hands, stopping her work. "That's fine. Thank you very much." He stood and faced her, confusion and hurt lining her face. "I'm sorry. It's just...with everything that's going on with, well, you know...I just didn't want to complicate things."

"Things are complicated. That's why I value our friendship."

He sat on the edge of his desk. "I take it things haven't improved between you and Bryce."

She shook her head. "He tries. Most of the time all I get from him is indifference. I've tried everything I can think of to get his attention, to make him fall in love with me again, but nothing works."

"Have you tried prayer?"

"I'm not much of a church-goer, Andy."

"It's not about going to church. It's about taking your problems to the Lord."

She chuckled. "I forgot you're a minister. Is that what helps you with Vanessa?"

He shook his head. "We're not going to get into my marriage. This is about you."

"That's the problem. The state of your marriage is key to the salvation or destruction of mine. If Bryce thinks there's a chance that he and Vanessa can be together, it's all over for us."

"Is that what you think?"

"Don't kid yourself, Andy. If Vanessa says the word, you're done. You and I will be the odd ones out." She shrugged. "I'm sorry. I didn't intend to come here and dump on you again."

"It's okay. I don't mind." He took her hand in his. "For the record, we are friends. You can dump on me anytime."

"You're sweet, Andy. Vanessa doesn't deserve you." She leaned in and kissed him gently on the lips. She reached up and stroked his cheek. "No," she whispered, "she doesn't deserve you at all." She kissed him again, this time letting her lips linger near his. She was surprised when he returned the kiss.

He jumped up. "I – I need to go back to work."

"I'm sorry. I should go." She turned away but he tugged on her hand.

"Wait, Regine. I do care about you. Another time, under different circumstances, I'd welcome the chance to be with you. But I'm committed to Vanessa. I can't, I won't betray her. And you should keep fighting for your marriage. Turning to another man, any man, is not the answer. I really do believe that God can restore it for you if you give him the chance." He released her hand and went to the other side of his desk.

"You're right." She smiled. "I'm sorry about the kiss. I should focus on getting things straight with my husband. I'm going to give that prayer thing a try." She walked out of the office but paused at the door. "Rain check on lunch?"

He nodded. "Most definitely."

~ ~ ~

Kendra was leaning on Regine's Mercedes Benz SUV when she exited the building. Arms folded, she scowled at a grinning Regine. "I'd like a word with you."

"I can see that," Regine responded. "Do you mind not leaning on my truck? I don't want the paint damaged."

Kendra ignored the dig. "I'm giving you fair warning. Stay away from Andy."

"What's your problem?"

"My problem is you, lady. I don't know what kind of game you're trying to run on him, but I'm telling you now, you'd better not hurt him."

"Is that so?" Regine crossed her arms and mirrored the other woman's stance. "And exactly what business is it of yours what happens to Andy? He's a grown man. He can take care of himself."

"I know Andy better than anyone except his mother. And I am telling you one last time to leave him alone."

"And if I don't?"

Kendra took a step forward and lowered her voice. "Don't let the degree and the fact that I'm a Christian fool you. You screw around Andy and this work we're doing and I promise you, you will regret the day your parents ever met." She took a step back. "Just so we understand each other."

"Oh, we understand each other all right. I thought Andy already had a wife."

Kendra reached back but before her hand made contact with Regine's face, she drew it closed into a fist. "We have worked too hard for too long to keep this mission going. These kids would be lost, or worse. I will do whatever I have to do to protect them and it. And as far as Andy and I are concerned, he is my friend——nothing more, nothing less."

"Andy's my friend, too," Regine replied. "Just so we understand each other." Without another word, she got into her truck and took off.

Kendra stood there, fuming. The lyrics to an old pop song crossed her mind. "She's going to emergency, and I'm going to jail," she muttered.

CHAPTER TWENTY-SIX

Shift

Vanessa scowled as she checked her appointments on her Blackberry. *Why this week? Why now?*

Jackson pulled up to the foundation's doors and let Vanessa out. She went in and headed directly to her assistant. "Mary, why is Bryce Harmon on my calendar today?"

"His company is presenting the new investment package to the board today."

"I'm aware of that, but why is Bryce coming?"

Mary shrugged. "I don't know. I got a call yesterday asking that his name be added to the guest list. Is something wrong?"

Vanessa shook her head and sighed. "No. I'm sorry I barked at you." *I should have anticipated this.* "I've got work to do. Unless my husband or Aunt Phoebe calls, I don't want to be disturbed until the meeting."

"Yes, ma'am. Is there anything I can do for you?"

Vanessa smiled. "No, thank you, Mary." She entered the office and closed the door behind her. She went to the desk and dropped her purse and briefcase. Slipping off her heels, she allowed her feet to ooze in the plushness of the carpet. Her mother had spared no expense when it came to the furnishing of the foundation's offices.

She crossed over to the mini-pantry in the corner, which was stocked with hot and cold beverages, fruit and snacks. Her mother also didn't like the idea of her assistant serving as her maid. Maris Carson felt that by showing off her domestic abilities, she could set her guests at ease while meeting with someone as powerful and well-connected as Maris Carson.

Vanessa made herself a cup of tea. Even though Carrie had made her eat a generous breakfast, Vanessa still found herself nibbling on a breakfast bar, something she did when she was under stress. *At this point, I'm going to gain ten pounds in a week.* She dropped the bar into the trash, picked up her teacup, and settled in at her desk.

Three hours later, Mary reminded her of the meeting. Vanessa straightened herself up, grabbed her portfolio, and headed for the boardroom. She greeted each member of the board, making small talk with them as Bryce and his associates continued their preparation for the meeting.

Everyone settled in as Bryce led the introductions and started the meeting. The presentation lasted just under an hour, with the board members peppering Bryce with questions. Once it was over, the board stayed behind to continue their discussion.

A half hour later, Vanessa emerged from the conference room and headed back to her office, but was cut off by Mary. "He's in there," she said.

"Who?"

"Bryce. Mr. Harmon. He said he had lunch plans with you. I didn't see it on your calendar, but he said he had spoken with you privately and you asked him to wait in your office."

Vanessa sighed, shaking her head. "He has some nerve," she muttered.

"Did I miss something?"

"No, not at all. I'll deal with him." She walked past Mary and continued into her office, closing the door. "I don't appreciate you lying to my assistant, Bryce."

He looked up from the sofa and smiled. "I didn't think you'd mind. Mary knows who I am."

"Still," she said, crossing over to her desk, "it puts her in an awkward position. Unless I've given her specific instructions, she's not supposed to let anyone into my office."

He grinned. "But I'm not just anyone. Mary knows that, too."

"She also knows I'm married. And your presence——your lies——only create confusion and fodder for the rumor mill. In the future, I'd appreciate it if you spoke to me first about any impromptu visits." She tossed her things on the desk and sat down. "Now what's this about lunch plans?"

"I wanted to see you, so I decided to take you to lunch."

"Bryce, I told you that we have to maintain discretion."

"No, what you told me is that you want to honor your vows. I respect that. But what's to stop us from having lunch together? I'm a financial adviser trying to woo a prospective client. We're old friends. It's a public setting. No one would suspect anything. It's completely on the up-and-up." He could see she was considering the idea. "C'mon, you have to eat."

"How do you know I don't have other plans for lunch?"

"I know you're not eating lunch with your husband. Regine said she was heading down to the mission to help out."

That settled it. Vanessa grabbed her purse. "Let's go."

~ ~ ~

As they settled into the lunch table, Bryce reached over and took Vanessa's hand. He gave it a gentle squeeze before she withdrew it. "Bryce, please," she whispered.

They gave their server their orders and settled back in their seats. "That was a very effective presentation you gave this morning. I think the board was definitely interested."

"I'm sure you had a lot to do with it," he replied.

"Not true. There are a lot of factors to consider. Your company definitely brought their A-game."

"We usually do. But it helps when we know we've got an in with our prospects."

She frowned. "You don't think that I'm going to just give you our business?"

"Well, you do exert a lot of influence on the board. I'm sure they would take your recommendation as confirmation."

"That's not how I see things. I'm just one vote overall."

"Yes, but your one vote will weigh heavily in our favor. The board will see that."

She shook her head. "I don't believe you. You think because of our relationship that I would unduly influence the foundation's board of directors just to throw some business your way?"

It was his turn to frown. "What's the problem? I thought we understood each other. The more business builds for me, the better the future for us." He leaned in and whispered, "I'll be in a better position to leave Regine so we can be together. Isn't that what you wanted?"

"That's irrelevant. You can't expect me to compromise my integrity——or the foundation's standing——just to finance your lifestyle," she hissed.

He leaned back in his seat. "He's gotten to you, hasn't he?"

"He who?"

"Andy. Your so-called husband."

"This has nothing to do with him."

"Doesn't it? Ever since the two of you got together, you've been riding this moral high horse and you don't seem to want to come down. Let me ask you something: where were your morals when we started seeing each other? Where were your principles when we made plans to be together?"

She took a sip of water before answering. Her insides were fluttering, but she was determined to keep her composure. "I'm not proud of the choices I've made. But I'm trying to do better, to do the right thing by everybody. And if you can't understand that, then you never really knew me." She stood. "I'm sorry about lunch. I seem to have lost my appetite." She turned and headed for the door.

The waiter arrived with their meals. "You can take that back," Bryce said. "My companion had other plans." He gave the waiter enough cash to cover the bill and tip, then left the restaurant.

CHAPTER TWENTY-SEVEN

Admission

Andy tossed and turned for more than an hour before finally deciding to get out of bed. The events of the day were still troubling him, despite having prayed and seeking forgiveness from the Lord. He couldn't pinpoint his uneasiness until he realized what he was feeling——guilt.

When he and Vanessa sat down to dinner, they both talked about their day. He never mentioned Regine's visit and their conversation, and the kiss they shared. As he spoke with Vanessa, he avoided making eye contact with her. He knew if he looked at her, he would have to confess everything. He couldn't bear the thought of her dealing with his betrayal.

"I'm in love with her," he muttered. "God help me, but I'm in love with Vanessa." He'd finally admitted to himself what he'd been afraid to say out loud. "The question now is how she feels about me."

Part of him wanted to run to her room and tell her how he felt. Then his brain kicked in; she probably would throw him out on his ear for disturbing her sleep. Better to have a conversation after a strong cup of coffee.

Since he couldn't sleep, he decided a warm cup of milk and a slice of Carrie's homemade devil's food cake was in order. He headed downstairs for his late night snack.

As he passed the library, he saw a light under the closed door. Who was up at this hour? He opened it and smiled at the sight——Adriana, asleep at the desk with her headphones still tucked in her ears. Careful not to disturb her, he went over and checked out the books she had on the desk: psychology and sociology texts, studies on the impact of violence and homelessness on inner city teens and families. Vanessa mentioned that the young woman was in college, but he had no idea what she was studying.

He nudged her awake and she jumped when she saw Andy standing over her. "Oh, Mr. Andy! I'm so sorry to disturb you. Mrs. Carson used to let me come in and study during my off hours. There's more space for my books and things than in my room." She started gathering her books. "I apologize. I'll get out of your way."

He waved his hands. "No, no. It's okay. I just wanted to see who was in here. What are you doing up so late?"

"What time is it?"

"Nearly one a.m."

She yawned and stretched. "I was sending out my resume."

"You're looking for another job?"

"No, an internship. Preferably a paid internship, but that's not likely." She noted his puzzled look, so she explained. "I have family in Mexico. I send most of my paycheck to them to live on. If I don't complete my internship, I can't graduate. But if I quit working here for my internship, I don't know how I will make it, and I will have nothing to send to mi familia."

"Nights are out because of your classes."

"Si, yes. You see my problem. So I come in at night and search for possible paid internships, hoping to get a jump on the competition. But it's too many people and too few positions. I don't know what I'm going to do."

Andy closed his eyes and lifted his hands in praise. Then he turned to a confused Adriana. "Print out a copy of your resume and give it to me in the morning."

"Why? Do you know somebody?"

"Of course——me! The mission is looking for interns. If you qualify, you can do your internship there and you'll still be able to have money to send to your family."

"But I will have to move out."

"Not necessarily. I'll work it out with Vanessa."

"Really? Gracias el Dio! Thank you Mr. Andy!" She jumped up and hugged him, then released him quickly and backed away.

Andy followed her gaze and turned to find Vanessa standing in the doorway. "What are you doing up this late?"

"I couldn't sleep," Vanessa replied. "I came down for a cup of tea. Looks like I'm in time for the party."

He frowned. "That's a cheap shot, Vanessa." He turned to Adriana. "Go on and get some sleep. We'll talk in the morning."

Adriana nodded her thanks and quickly gathered her books and papers. She excused herself to Vanessa who remained in place. "So what did I miss?"

"What did you hear?"

"Only that you told her she wouldn't have to move out and that you'd work something out with me."

"True. I was going to bring it up at breakfast."

"I'm up now. Tell me what's going on."

"It's nothing lascivious, I can assure you."

"Lascivious? You really are a preacher. No one else uses that word except preachers."

"At least you get my drift." He crossed over and took her by the arm. "I'll explain everything over a cup of tea and a piece of cake."

CHAPTER TWENTY-EIGHT

Thanksgiving

Though initially reluctant, Vanessa warmed to the idea of letting Adriana complete her internship but still live in the mansion. They found a temporary maid to handle Adriana's duties during the week and Adriana worked the weekends.

Kendra was also pleased to have Adriana's help, especially since she didn't have to do all the work of looking for her. The two women hit it off beautifully and Adriana eagerly jumped into her role.

By the time Thanksgiving rolled around, everyone was ready for a break. As was tradition, Andy and Kendra, with Adriana's help, got the mission ready for their annual Thanksgiving dinner. Andy was preparing a list of caterers to use to give his volunteer cooks a break, but Carrie objected. "Nonsense," she told him. "Those children need a home cooked meal."

"Most of their meals are home cooked," Andy said. "At least, they are kitchen-cooked."

"But they've never had one done by me."

"Carrie, you can't handle all that cooking for over fifty people."

"Baby please. I've cooked for more than that plenty of times. Besides, I'll have help."

"Who?"

"Those children. Most of them are old enough to get into the kitchen and fix their own food. What they don't know, I'll teach 'em. I'll be good experience when they get out on their own." She grinned. "Matter of fact, Andy, I've been thinking about something. For your children."

"What's that?"

"I'd like to offer them a cooking class once a week. On my day off, of course."

"I couldn't ask you to do that, Carrie."

"You didn't ask, I volunteered. Besides, it would give me something to do on the weekends other than just sitting up in my room getting stiff. I can teach them how to make good, nutritious meals. And who knows? Maybe they can get hired on as a cook or become 'The Next Food Network Star' or something."

He hugged the older woman. "Thank you, Ms. Carrie. God bless you, sweetheart."

"Oh, you go on. Let me be so I can get my list together."

~ ~ ~

The Thanksgiving dinner at the mission was a hit. The residents that helped prepare the meal eagerly volunteered for Carrie's weekend cooking classes.

Vanessa joined Ella and the volunteer serving/cleanup crew, which included Adriana and several of the foundation's board members who were impressed with the facility. Sis. Freeman also showed up, but was clearly more interested in whatever gossip she could dig up.

The real surprise was Aunt Phoebe's arrival. She had already made plans to have dinner with friends, so Vanessa and Andy were shocked when she appeared on the arm of Alexander Nichols, the family attorney.

"Aunt Phoebe!" Vanessa exclaimed, hugging her great-aunt. "This is a surprise. I thought you were having dinner with the Kellermans in Northbrook."

"I did. But listening to Betty Kellerman's story about her gallbladder surgery for the fiftieth time was much more than I could bear. I told her we had accidentally double-booked and we needed to spend time here."

"You've never double-booked anything, ever."

"I know that, but Betty was already loaded before the appetizers had come. She didn't seem to mind a bit. Besides, I really wanted to be with family today of all days."

"We're glad to have you," Andy said, coming up beside her and giving her a quick squeeze. He shook hands with Alexander and said, "Why don't you both come sit down? We'll get you something to eat."

"Nonsense," Phoebe replied. "I came to help. What can I do?"

"You can rest, Aunt Phoebe. Alexander, will you tell her?"

The other man shrugged. "You think I can change her mind? Anyway, I'd love to help out if I can." He patted his bulging stomach. "It'll do me some good to work up a sweat."

"About all that's left is clean-up duty in the kitchen."

"Sounds good to me. Maybe Carrie will fix me a plate, too." He headed in the direction Andy pointed to.

"What about me?" Phoebe asked.

"We were just about to serve dessert," Vanessa replied.

"Lead the way."

~ ~ ~

At the end of the evening, the volunteers sat at the table enjoying seconds. All except for Phoebe, who was sitting in a corner, quietly conversing with one of the residents, a single teenage mother with a toddler and an infant. Phoebe was rocking the baby in her arms as the young mother tried to calm her toddler down.

"That's a sight I never thought I'd see," Vanessa said, leaning her head on Andy's shoulder.

"What's that?"

"Aunt Phoebe holding a baby."

"Why does that surprise you? I'm sure she held you as a baby."

"I don't know. She's never struck me as the maternal type. Don't get me wrong. She's a very loving woman, but she's not the kind of person that you'd curl up next to if you were sick or upset."

"Maybe getting older has softened her up."

"Maybe." She sighed. "I'm exhausted, but in a good way, you know?"

"I know how you feel. These days drain me physically, but my spirit is lifted seeing these kids having fun and enjoying themselves the way I did as a kid. Thanksgiving was always a big deal in our family, all the cousins and aunts and uncles getting together."

"You don't do it now?"

"Nope. My family has scattered around the globe. Getting them all together would take an act of God. But being here makes up for it."

The unruly toddler had finally settled down in his mother's lap and was drifting off to sleep. Phoebe stood and headed over to the table with the baby still nestled in her arms. She sat down across from the couple. "That is a remarkable young woman over there," she said.

"Kinisha," Andy said, nodding. "Yeah, she is pretty special."

"In spite of all that she's been through, she is determined to do right by her children and herself."

"I know." He turned to Vanessa to explain. "When Kinisha got pregnant, her parents put her out and told her if she kept the baby, she couldn't come back home. She moved in with the baby's father's family. She kept going to school, got her high school diploma, and finished in the top 20 of her class. She enrolled in college. When she got pregnant again, the boyfriend turned abusive, accusing her of cheating on him. He beat her until she finally found the courage to run away. She hid with friends and wound up here after the baby was born."

"That's terrible," Vanessa said.

"Yet she hasn't given up on her future. She works when she can and takes online college classes at night. She wants to be an engineer. She's got the smarts to do it, but she just can't catch a break."

"What about scholarships?"

"She got several, but with two kids, she can't afford to go to school full-time."

"She needs more than scholarships," Phoebe declared. "She needs child care and a decent place to live. I'm going to see that she gets it."

"What are you talking about?"

"She's going to the University of Chicago."

"Even with her scholarships, she can't afford that school."

"And what about housing and child care?" Vanessa asked.

"I'm going to set her up in an apartment with nanny services. And when the children are old enough, they can be enrolled in the University's Lab School. I'm going to cover those expenses personally. The University will take care of the rest of her tuition and fees."

"How can you be sure about that?"

"Because I'm good friends with their board chairman. He and I will sit down and discuss it and we'll arrange everything."

"Phoebe, that's a generous offer."

"It's nothing, Andy. If there's one thing I cannot stand, it's to see a bright mind go to waste for lack of an opportunity. I have been very blessed over the years. I can afford to be a blessing to someone who truly deserves it." She stood and went back to sit with Kinisha and her sleeping toddler.

"I guess we're done," Andy said, chuckling.

"You know Aunt Phoebe. When her mind's made up, there is no discussion." She tried to stifle a yawn, but failed. "I'm sorry. I didn't realize how tired I was."

Andy stood and pulled her to her feet. "It's been a long day. Hard work can exhaust you when you're not used to doing it," he said, grinning.

"Hey!" She punched him in his arm. "Low blow."

"Sorry. I couldn't help myself." He wrapped her arm around his and escorted her out of the dining room. "Thanks for all this," he said, quietly.

"All what?"

"This——the funding, the dinner. You."

"Me?"

"Yes." He stopped and turned to face her. "I know that a lot of this is because of our deal. But for you to be here today, to really take an active part in this ministry, it really meant a lot to those kids. And to me." He leaned in and kissed her on the lips.

When they parted, he saw the hesitation in her eyes, so he stepped back, but she drew him closer. "Andy, I didn't give up my holiday as part of our deal. I did it because I wanted to be with you. Even if it meant sharing you with the mission. They're a part of your heart." She reached up and stroked his face. "I hope I'm a part of your heart, too."

She wrapped her arms around his neck and pulled him in for a kiss. This one was far more deep and passionate. He didn't hesitate, his own desire matching hers. It was familiar, yet different, as their decade-long passion reignited.

A clearing of a throat interrupted them. Reluctantly, they pulled back and turned to find Alexander standing there grinning. "I'm sorry to interrupt, but Phoebe is ready to head home. I came to see if you wished to ride with us, Vanessa."

Before she could respond, Andy spoke. "That's probably a good idea. I have to stay until the night crew gets here then I've got to get my mom home." Seeing her confusion, he said, "I'll see you at home. We'll talk. I promise." He leaned down and gave her a quick peck on the lips and headed towards his office.

Vanessa didn't move. *What just happened?*

CHAPTER TWENTY-NINE

Misfire

On the ride home, Vanessa got a call from Andy letting her know that he was going to be late getting home as his night staff was delayed. Disappointed, but determined, Vanessa decided that one way or another, she was going to force Andy to tell her how he felt about her.

Ever since their "honeymoon," they had danced around the subject of their feelings, dropping hints, but never really coming forward and saying out loud their innermost thoughts.

Vanessa knew how she felt——she was in love with Andy. But she was afraid to push him, especially if he didn't feel the same way. If she were truly honest, she'd have admitted she never stopped loving Andy.

After tonight's kiss, it was clear that he had feelings, strong feelings, for her. As far as she was concerned, their talk was only going to end one way——with her in his arms and in his bed.

Arriving home, she headed to her room. She prepared a long, soothing bubble bath, complete with her favorite bath oil and signature scented candles. After soaking for a while, she climbed out and added body butter that head the same scent as her bath oil and candles.

Her final decision was what to wear. She didn't want to show him that she was too eager, but she wanted to convey that she was prepared to fulfill her marital role in every way possible. She settled on an ivory silk charmeuse cami pajama set, with a matching peignoir. The cami was just fitted enough to expose her décolletage without appearing to be easy; yet it was simple enough to remove should things progress as she anticipated.

After dressing, she settled in her chaise lounge with a book in her hand and prayer in her heart.

~ ~ ~

The sound of running water awakened her. Vanessa stood and stretched, then glanced at the clock. It was nearly 1:30 a.m. *How long has Andy been home? Did he come in and find me asleep? Crap!*

She heard the water cut off. Time to make her move. She quickly brushed her teeth, checked her hair——her bob had grown out and the layered cut was shaped so well she didn't need to curl it——added a touch of lip gloss, and headed down the hall.

She tried to think of what to say to him, then decided it was better if she started with small talk and let him make the first move. He did kiss her first, after all.

As she got to the door, she heard his voice. It's much too late for him to be on the phone. She tapped lightly on the door. When he didn't answer, she opened it and stuck her heard around the door.

Andy was kneeling at his bedside, clad only in his pajama bottoms. She could see the tension in his back as his muscles clenched with each prayerful word. The other thing she noticed was his wedding ring laying on the bed in front of him. "I can't do this, Lord," he muttered. "I just can't keep doing this to Vanessa. It isn't fair to either one of us."

That was all she needed to hear. Vanessa stepped back and closed the door. With tears forming, she tiptoed back to her room and shut the door. The kiss had been a mistake; Andy's words made that clear. She quickly changed out of the silk pajamas and into her customary cotton pajamas and climbed into bed. She sobbed in her pillow as she realized that she was going to lose the love of her life——again.

CHAPTER THIRTY

Unspoken

The next morning, Andy strolled into the kitchen where he found Carrie humming to herself as she cooked over the stove. He stood next to her, wrapped an arm round her shoulders, and gave her a kiss on the check. "You are an amazing woman, Ms. Carrie. Yesterday was perfect."

She just smiled. "I was more than happy to do it. I haven't had that much fun in a long time."

"Fun! That was a lot of work!"

"Hmmph." She waved him away with her spatula. "That's nothing. I've whipped up dinners much larger than that and for much fancier clientele."

He took a seat on the other side of the island. "Speaking of whipping up stuff, what are you doing cooking this morning? I thought we gave you the weekend off."

"For what? My family is right here. I don't like shopping in those crazy crowds. Besides, I'm happiest in the kitchen. Gives me time to talk to the Lord. And we've been having a mighty good talk this morning." She pulled out a plate and served up a helping of grits, eggs, bacon, sausage, and biscuits and put it in front of him.

He blessed the food and began eating. "Ms. Carrie, I do believe this is your calling. Good thing we have a gym around here; otherwise, I wouldn't get through the door."

Carrie laughed. "You could stand to gain a few pounds. I know how hard you work. And after talking to Kendra yesterday, I know that you don't eat enough when you're at work. She told me that you almost always skip lunch and I know you don't each much breakfast when you go in."

"I do okay."

"Hmmph. She's worried about you. So is your mother."

"You talked to my mother?"

"Yes. She's worried about you and so am I. but I've been talking to the Lord about you——you and Miss Vanessa. So I know everything is going to be all right."

"Speaking of Vanessa, where is she?"

Carrie shook her head. "She said she had work to do at the office."

"But you didn't believe her?"

"No. I thought she might have gone shopping, but she looked terrible."

He put down his fork. "What do you mean?"

She sighed. "I've known Miss Vanessa practically her whole life. She has never left this house without being completely put together. But this morning, she was in an old jogging suit, hair pulled up, and no makeup. And she looked like she hadn't slept all night."

"I wonder what was bothering her."

She pointed a finger at him. "You."

"Me?"

"Yes, you."

"What did she say? Did she mention me specifically?"

"Not in so many words. It's more of what she didn't say."

"What do you mean?"

"When I asked her if the two of you had plans today, she got this funny look on her face and sort of stiffened up. Then she said, 'Andy and I don't have any plans together. At all.' Then she just left."

Andy leaned back in his seat. He had hoped to talk to Vanessa, but it was so late when he came in and he didn't want to disturb her. He showered and went to his knees in prayer, seeking clearer direction about his relationship with her. By the time he finished, he knew it was time to come clean about his feelings with his wife. He went to her bedroom, but she was fast asleep. Now she was gone and from Carrie's words, clearly perturbed at him. He decided he would settle things with her once and for all when she returned.

~ ~ ~

With a rare day off, Andy took advantage of the Carson's extensive library to do some studying. After a quick lunch, he decided to catch up on a couple of old black and white films on one of the cable channels.

It was nearly dark by the time Vanessa returned home. He greeted her at the door and helped her with the many bags she carried in. "You must have worked really hard today. I didn't realize the foundation had its own mall," he said, chuckling.

"What's the point of having money if you don't spend it?" she countered. "At least I used it wisely. There were too many great sales to pass up."

"Really? What did you get me?" He began poking through the bags when she slapped his hands away.

"I didn't get you anything. You'll have to wait until Christmas to see if Santa brings you anything."

"'If?' Okay, fine. In any case, I'm glad you're back. I want to talk to you."

"Me, too. They say shopping is retail therapy and I had a lot of time to think."

"About?"

"About us. Last night was a mistake. The kiss, I mean, was a mistake."

"A mistake?"

"Yes. It's clear we still have a connection. But we have an arrangement. A business arrangement. And our making it personal will only complicate things."

"Complicate things? You're right about us having a connection. But why would discussing what happened complicate things? Why can't we make it personal between us?"

"Because it's not what I want."

"Really?" He took a step forward, but she retreated back a step. "What do you want?"

"I want us to continue with the way things were, with us being friends, nothing more. I want us to fulfill the terms of our agreement and then part ways. Simple. Uncomplicated."

"What if I want complicated?"

"I'm sorry. It's just the way things have to be." She gathered her bags and headed upstairs.

Andy started to follow her but thought better of it. From her tone, it was clear that she had made up her mind. He was not about to let Vanessa Carson break his heart once again. *If that's the way she wants it, I'm more than happy to play my part. Even if it kills me.*

CHAPTER THIRTY-ONE

Suitable

The next two weeks made for a delicate balancing act for Vanessa and Andy. They rarely spent any time alone together, but continued to make public appearances as warranted, putting up a front as a happily married couple.

At home, however, the only time they saw each other was at meals. Carrie insisted they eat together when they were home. Their conversations were limited to small talk. The cordiality they started with after Thanksgiving soon gave way to comfortable, even friendly bantering. Still, they made it a point to avoid physical contact whenever possible.

~ ~ ~

The holiday season was in full gear as Andy and Vanessa prepared for the Carson Foundation annual winter gala. Andy had tried to avoid going, but his wife insisted. "All the foundation's recipients will be there. It would look bad if my husband, whose mission happens to benefit due to the foundation, did not attend."

"Okay, okay. I'll be there."

"Good. I'm inviting Kendra and her guest as well."

"Really?"

"Of course. She does so much to help keep the mission running. Besides, since you'll be with me, it'll make more sense to have her represent the mission in all the PR photos. She knows as much about the place as you do."

"I don't know how she'll feel about all the pictures, but she definitely deserves a night out."

~ ~ ~

Andy stood in the mirror, shaking his head. Vanessa had insisted he wear a tux to the party. She went with him to the store to help him pick it out. It was probably the most time they had spent alone together in weeks.

~ ~ ~

They agreed on a black Calvin Klein three-button tux that fit him well. He insisted on paying for it himself, but balked at the price. She just smiled and pulled out her American Express card, handing it to the sales manager. She put her hands on his shoulders and peered at him in the mirror. "You're my husband, Andy. Like it or not, you are a part of the Carson family. You need to look like you belong. Besides, you deserve something nice for yourself."

"I understand what you're saying, but this is too much. For what you're spending on this suit, I could pay the shelter's utilities for a month or purchase food. It's too much."

She dropped her hands and took a step back. "It's too much? Or I'm too much?"

He saw the tension in her posture. "No. I'm sorry. I appreciate what you're doing." He turned to face her. "I appreciate everything you've done. I do. It's just... it's a lot of money for a suit I probably won't wear again. You know my normal attire is usually jeans or khakis and a shirt. Other than dressing for church, I have nowhere to wear this."

She pursed her lip and clasped her hands. "Think of this as an investment. The mission is attracting a lot of attention from potential donors. Wealthy donors. You're probably going to be called upon to attend events like our holiday party. A quality tuxedo like this will last for years. You can dress it up or down." She turned away. "And who knows? Maybe you'll wear it to your next wedding," she muttered, rummaging through her purse.

He shrugged. "I guess you're right. But at least let me pay for half."

"Suit yourself; no pun intended."

~ ~ ~

Now staring at himself in his bedroom mirror, he had to admit Vanessa was right. The tux had been altered to fit him exactly. The lines and fit were perfect. "Not bad. Not bad at all."

He glanced at his watch, and then headed out the door. In the hallway, he called out, "Vanessa, if we're going to get to the hotel in time, we need to leave in ten minutes. We still have to pick up my mom."

"I'll be down shortly," she called out.

The doorbell rang. He jogged down the stairs and arrived just as Dora opened the front door. "Mom! What are you doing here? I told you we would pick you up." He hugged her and gave her a kiss on the cheek.

"I decided to come and beat the storm." She took a step back and took an appreciative glance at her son. "My, my. You do clean up nice."

Andy grinned. The line from an old sitcom popped in his head. "Well, you know, what can I say?" He took a quick spin, pivoting like a model on a runway. "Don't hate me because I'm beautiful."

"No," Ella said, looking up. "She's beautiful."

He turned and looked toward the top of the stairs where Vanessa stood. Once again, her presence left him speechless. He stood transfixed as she descended the stairs. Her black silk gown hugged her body, accentuating her curvaceous figure, yet the bottom of her dress floated around her as she walked. Swarovski crystals glistened against the light, providing a shimmering effect that centered at her hip. The bodice had a slight sweetheart neckline, which wrapped around her shoulders asymmetrically. Gentle curvy waves of hair framed her face. She'd opted for a simple crystal teardrop necklace with matching earrings and bracelet.

At the bottom of the stairs, Vanessa gave Ella a gentle hug. "We were on our way to pick you up."

"No need. You look lovely, Vanessa."

"Thank you." She turned to Andy, who was staring at her, dumbfounded.

Ella cleared her throat, breaking Andy out of his daze. He blinked, and then turned to his mother, who arched her eyebrows and nodded in her daughter-in-law's direction.

"Oh. Uh..." He turned to his wife. "You're stunning."

She smiled. "Thank you. You don't look too shabby yourself."

"I had help." He grinned. They continued to stare at each other, smiles growing wider as the seconds passed.

Ella chuckled, and then took off her coat. "You two are so silly."

Vanessa's grin faded. "Ella! You're not dressed."

"That's because I'm not going."

"Why not? Are you okay?" Andy asked.

"I'm fine."

"If you're not going, what are you doing here?"

"I'm here to keep Phoebe company." As if on cue, Phoebe emerged from the sitting area.

"Ella! Glad you could make it. Andy, Vanessa, you both look wonderful. But it's getting late. Shouldn't you be going?"

"The question is, why aren't you going, Aunt Phoebe?" Vanessa asked. "Everyone will be expecting you."

"Give them my regrets. I wanted to spend the evening in. Ella was gracious enough to join me. I think Carrie and Dora may join us for an evening of bid whist."

"Since when do you play cards?"

"Since I've had someone to play with." She went and took Ella by the arm. "Have a wonderful time, you two. Come, let's get warm by the fire. Carrie has a lovely dinner prepared for us." The two women walked away, leaving the couple perplexed.

"Did you know about this?" Vanessa asked.

"I had no idea," Andy replied. He shrugged. "I guess it really doesn't matter. They're not going. But we should get going." He went over to the foyer closet, pulled out her mink, and held it out for her. He assisted her in putting on the coat, and then grabbed his. "You really do look beautiful." He extended his arm to her. "Shall we go?"

She wrapped her arm around his and they walked out the door to the waiting limo.

CHAPTER THIRTY-TWO

Expectations

Light fluffy snow fell on the guests arriving at the Peninsula Hotel, just a block off Chicago's famed Magnificent Mile. The entrance was lined with local and national media, taking photos of the guests arriving at the foundation's gala. Inside, Andy and Vanessa greeted the guests warmly as they entered the lounge for the cocktail hour.

Andy's face brightened when he saw Kendra enter, escorted by a tall, handsome young man. Before he could ask, Kendra provided the introductions. "Andy, Vanessa, I'd like you to meet my, um, boyfriend, Doctor Ben Sheppard. Ben, this is Andy and Vanessa Carson-Perry, our hosts."

They couples shook hands. "It's a pleasure to finally meet you both," Ben said. "I've heard so much about you. I really admire the work of the foundation and what you're doing at the mission."

"It's nice to meet you too, Ben," Andy replied. He raised a quizzical brow at his assistant director, which she ignored.

"So this is Ben? No wonder you've been keeping him a secret," Vanessa said, grinning.

"Only from people I work with who are incredibly overprotective," Kendra replied, turning her narrowed glare towards Andy.

He shrugged. "I can't help it. Call it the big brother instinct. Besides, I can't let anything happen to you. The whole place would fall completely apart without you."

"True. But for tonight, it's in Adriana's very capable hands."

"Exactly," Vanessa said. "So go in and enjoy yourselves."

As the couple departed, Andy turned to his wife, barely concealing his grin. "Kendra has a boyfriend!"

"I know! Isn't that wonderful?"

"Maybe. I'll have to get more information on him." A thought occurred to him. "Wait. You said, 'So this is Ben,' like you already knew he was coming. How long have you known about this guy?"

"Since Thanksgiving. Kendra and I were talking while we were doing the dishes. He sounds like a good guy. Plus, he's gorgeous."

"I wouldn't say gorgeous."

"Nor should you."

"So what's his story? What did she tell you?"

"Let it go, Andy. She's a grown woman and perfectly able to take care of herself. She doesn't strike me as the type of woman to fall for a fool. You should know that better than anyone."

"You're right I guess. Still..." He stiffened as he saw Bryce and Regine entering the foyer. He touched his wife's elbow and noticed that she too had gone rigid.

Despite her feelings, Vanessa greeted the couple cordially. "I'm glad the two of you could make it."

"Oh, we wouldn't have missed it," Regine said, keeping her eyes on Andy. "Bryce had second thoughts, but I insisted that we come. We just couldn't miss out on the party of the season."

"I hope the party lives up to your expectations."

"Oh, no doubt. It promises to be a most interesting evening." She wrapped her arm around her husband's and tugged him towards the cocktail area.

"That's for sure," Andy muttered.

CHAPTER THIRTY-THREE

Dancing

Everyone seemed to be enjoying the delicious food and spectacular wine. The live jazz ensemble kept the tempo at a smooth pace but played soft enough to allow guests to have conversations with each other. Near the end of the dinner hour, Vanessa stood to give her speech.

"Good evening and welcome to the Carson Foundation holiday party. I hope you are having a great time," Vanessa said. "There will be lots more fun, once I get through this speech." She waited until the laughter died down before continuing.

"Besides the three worthy organizations we are honoring tonight, we are here to present the recipients of the Matthew and Maris Carson scholarship. As you know, we have applicants from all over the country, all incredibly brilliant and talented. We narrowed down our applicants to three winners.

"Victoria Robinson has a 4.5 GPA, carrying three Advanced Placement classes in literature, economics, and biology, is editor of her school newspaper, and a member of her church's drama club. Victoria is heading to Harvard, where she will double major in journalism and finance. Hoping to follow in the footsteps of her father, Richard, and her mother, the acclaimed author Daphine Robinson, Victoria has decided to create her own publishing house, specializing in marketing first-time authors of color." Vanessa extended her hand, and a young light-skinned woman with long locs stood. She grinned shyly, then waved as she took in the applause.

Vanessa continued as Victoria took her seat. "Matthew Cooper has an amazing story. Raised by his grandparents, Matthew has had perfect attendance since kindergarten and has been on the honor roll every year. As a young child, Matthew had two passions——drumming and preaching. In addition to his studies, Matthew has been a Sunday school teacher, a mentor to young kids, and has started his own Christian jazz band. Additionally, Matthew has spent his summers on mission trips to Haiti and the Dominican Republic, bringing the gospel and good music as well as organizing food and supplies. Matthew is headed to the University of Chicago, majoring in theology and music education. His desire is to open a conservatory of music and bring the gospel to all nations." The lanky young man nodded his head appreciatively and took his seat.

"Cayla Richardson is the valedictorian of her senior class, president of the student government association, and is taking AP classes in Biology and Chemistry. Additionally, she plays volleyball and is a member of the Big Brothers/Big Sisters organization. Cayla is heading to Howard University as a pre-med student, with a concentration in either pediatric cardiology or pediatric neurology. Join me as we congratulate these three deserving recipients in wishing them nothing but success." She joined in the applause and beamed as the young woman took her seat.

Vanessa waited until the applause subsided before continuing. "Making the transition from high school to college is an important step in a young person's life. But it's only when we take our first steps into the world as adults do we really gain perspective on what life is all about. It's then we can appreciate the sacrifices our parents have made for us. It's then we can understand why they pushed us, why they demanded so much from us. It's only then that we see what our responsibility is to the generation that comes after us."

She paused and looked down at her hands. Blinking back tears, she continued. "This has been a year of transition for me. While I have been of age for a minute now," she could hear the chuckles in the audience, "I can honestly say that this past year was the year I grew up. When my father passed, I leaned on my mother and my aunt. They were the grown-ups. They handled the business of this family. But when my mother became ill,

I had to become the grown-up. I had to, as Paul so aptly stated in First Corinthians, 'put away childish things.' My mother, my aunt, this very foundation depended on me to be the grown up, to handle the business of the family. It was inevitable, I guess, but still, I didn't want to be the grown-up.

"But I did. And I am the grown-up. And it's only now that I can appreciate those things that my parents taught me. I appreciate the work that they did for others. I appreciate the love that they gave me freely, unconditionally. Their spirit is a part of me. And I hope to continue not only their work, but their legacy of service. Thank you all so much for coming tonight. On behalf of the Carson Foundation, I wish you all love and peace during this holiday season. Thank you and may God bless you. Enjoy the rest of your evening!" She turned as she saw Andy stand up and applaud, leading everyone in the room to do the same. As she went to her seat, he pulled her into an embrace and kissed her on the cheek.

"That was beautiful," he whispered.

"Thanks." She smiled and took a slight bow as her guests wrapped up their applause.

Pam came over. "Let's get the photos done now while dessert is being served."

"Excuse me, Andy," Vanessa said.

"Sure."

"No, you're coming too," Pam said.

"No one wants a photograph with me."

"No, but everyone wants a photograph with the happy couple. So come on."

~ ~ ~

The dancing kicked off with Andy and Vanessa leading the way. The band played a mid-tempo number by Anita Baker, and Andy drew Vanessa close. "What are you doing?" she whispered in his ear, careful to keep a smile on her face.

"I'm dancing with my wife," he replied.

"But why are you holding me so close? Everybody is looking at us."

"That's the point, isn't it? We're supposed to be a happily married couple. Newlyweds, in case you've forgotten. It would be weird if we were dancing like strangers." When she didn't respond, he said, "You've been so distant lately, ever since we kissed Thanksgiving night."

"Why are you bringing this up now?" she hissed, the plastered smile faltering.

"Because I want to know what's wrong. What happened? I know that kiss wasn't one-sided. Was I mistaken?"

"No."

"Then what? Talk to me, Vanessa. I thought we were on the verge of something."

"On the verge of making a very big mistake."

The song ended and she pulled away to applaud the band. As they began a slower number, she turned to leave, but Andy grabbed her by the hand, then pulled her back to him. "It wasn't a mistake, Vanessa. I don't believe that. I believe God brought us together to give us a second chance. In fact, I know it in my heart."

Tears formed in her eyes as her emotions swirled within her. He sounded so sincere; yet, she couldn't forget the words she heard pouring out of him that night: I can't do this, Lord...I just can't keep doing this. "I can't deal with this now, Andy."

"Okay, I understand. Wrong place, wrong time. But we need to have that talk——tonight."

She nodded, unsure of the steadiness of her voice. He kissed her hand then released her. She did her best not to run out of the ballroom. Once she made it to the foyer, she headed directly for the ladies' room. She found the stall farthest from the entrance, locked herself in, sat down, and allowed the tears to stream down her face.

CHAPTER THIRTY-FOUR

Trouble

After posing for photos with Kendra, Andy left the ballroom and found a seat on a bench in a corner of the foyer. He mentally kicked himself. Of all the times to bring up the state of their relationship, he probably had the worst timing in the world. This had not gone the way he had planned.

"Quarter for your thoughts."

He looked up to see Kendra standing over him. "I don't think they're worth that much." He smiled. "You look really nice tonight. Did I tell you that?"

She spun around. The form-fitting chocolate gown shimmered in the glow of the lights. "No. But I'll take the compliment." She sat down next to him. "So?"

"So, Ben seems like a nice guy. What's the story?"

"He's a doctor just wrapping up his residency at Northwestern. We met at a friend's birthday party. And before you ask, the reason I hadn't said anything to you——not that it's really any of your business——is because with both of our crazy schedules, we haven't really had all that much time to connect. We've only had time in the last month or so to spend any quality time together."

"That's nice."

She nudged him. "Talk."

"About?"

"Whatever's eating you. If I had to guess, based on what I know and what I saw, I'd say it has something to do with your bride."

"You guessed wisely."

"So?"

"So, I think I may lose her."

"What? Why?"

"Because I love her."

"Whoa! That's great, isn't it?" When he shook his head, she asked, "Why is this a problem?"

"Because I don't know if she feels the same. I think I've scared her off."

"Have you told her how you feel?"

"Not in those words."

Kendra huffed. "Men. How clueless are you? You need to get in her face and tell her how you feel! You need to tell her that you're in love with her."

"What if she doesn't feel the same way?"

"Oh, she does. Trust me."

~ ~ ~

Vanessa emerged from the stall, blowing her nose. As she headed for the sink, she was acutely aware she was no longer alone. She was grateful to see Pam standing at the vanity with her makeup bag. "How did you know where I was?" she asked.

"I saw you leave after your dance with Andy. I followed you." She handed Vanessa a paper towel. "Talk to me. What's going on with the two of you?"

"I don't know."

Pam sighed. "Let me guess. You fell in love with him."

She nodded. "I guess I never really stopped loving him."

"This is good! That means your marriage is for real!"

"Shhh!" Vanessa glanced around.

"There's no one else in here. I had one of the staff hang an out of order sign on the door."

"You're good."

"Yes, I am, and don't try to change the subject. You're in love with your husband."

"Yes."

"Is he in love with you?"

"I don't know."

"What do you mean, you don't know?"

"I mean I don't know! One minute he's kissing me and telling me we need to 'talk' and the next he's saying he can't bear to be with me."

"Hold up, wait a minute. He kissed you? When did this happen?"

"You mean the last time?"

"There's been more than one?"

"Yes, but I'm not getting into it. This last time was on Thanksgiving. We kissed, and it wasn't just a peck on the lips. This was the real deal. The way we used to kiss back in the day before we broke up."

"But you said he said he couldn't bear to be with you."

"Yes."

"He said that to you?"

"Not exactly."

"Then what did he say?"

She shrugged. "It's not that he said it, but he said he was being unfair to me."

"Unfair about what?"

"I don't know."

Pam groaned. This conversation was exasperating. "Why didn't you ask him what he meant?"

"Because he was praying."

"Praying?" Pam slapped the marble sink. "You are killing me, Vanessa, you know that? First, you run off and get married. Now, you tell me you're in love with him and he's kissing you, but he's never said he loves you." She shook her head. "You need to go talk to him. Right now."

"But the party——"

"Screw the party! I saw the way the two of you were dancing. That man is in love with you. And if you don't do something about it, you're going to lose him—— again. How many chances do you think you're going to get with this guy?"

"What if he doesn't feel the same?"

"Then at least you'll have your answer."

Vanessa sighed. "I guess you're right." She turned for the door, but Pam blocked her.

"Oh, no, my sister. There's no way you're leaving out of here looking like that."

Vanessa turned to look at herself in the mirror, then burst out laughing. "I wouldn't want me looking like this!"

Pam opened her makeup bag. "Let's get it together before you go public." She began fixing Vanessa's hair as Vanessa reapplied her makeup. After a few minutes, Pam declared, "Perfect! Now go get your man!"

Vanessa gave her friend a quick hug and they opened the door. Vanessa stopped when she saw Bryce standing in the corridor.

Pam stepped forward. "This isn't a good time, Bryce."

He ignored her. "Vanessa. I just need a few minutes of your time. Please."

Vanessa stepped around Pam. "I don't think there's anything more to be said."

"I think there's a lot more to be said."

"Vanessa needs to mingle with her guests," Pam interjected.

"Please, Vanessa. I promise not to be more than a few minutes. You can at least give me that."

Before Pam could object, Vanessa squeezed her arm. "It's okay, Pam." She turned to Bryce. "You're right. I owe you that much."

"Five minutes, and not a second more," Pam said, scowling. She glared at Bryce before walking away.

Vanessa waited until Pam was out of earshot before speaking. "I'm surprised you even came after the way we left things."

"I've tried to do the right thing," Bryce said. "I've respected your wishes and stayed away from you. I've tried to focus on my marriage. Things haven't been going well. I just wanted to talk to you one last time to see if we can make it work for us."

~ ~ ~

Kendra and Andy turned when Regine walked up to them. "Good evening, Kendra. Don't you look lovely," she said, smiling brightly. "Andy, may I speak with you for a moment, privately?"

Kendra crossed her arms and fixed a stern look on her face. Before she could say anything, Andy replied, "Sure, Regine. We're done."

Kendra frowned at him but stood. "Yes, I suppose I should go and find my guy. Remember what I said, Andy." She started to leave, but as she got behind Regine's back, she turned and mouthed, "Watch out for her."

Andy chuckled as Kendra plastered a smile on her face and waved when Regine quickly turned around. Regine turned back towards Andy. "May I sit?"

"Please." He gestured towards a spot next to him. "So how are you enjoying your evening so far?"

"Everything has been just wonderful," she replied. "Simply divine. But I wouldn't have expected anything less from Vanessa Carson."

"You've been to many of these?"

"A few." She sighed. "I've missed you, Andy. I've missed our friendship." She moved her hand to cover his, but he eased it away.

"I'm sorry about that, Regine. It's just, last time we saw each other..."

"I remember. I remember it well." She turned away as a tear rolled down her cheek. "I was so embarrassed. Especially in light of everything that was going on in my marriage."

"How are things between you and Bryce?"

She shook her head. "Nothing's changed. I did what you said, tried to turn my marriage around. But it's hard when only one person really works at it."

"But that's the thing, Regine. If you stand faithful, God will reward you."

She turned back to face him. "Reward me? With what, a divorce?" At his shocked expression, she laughed. "Don't be so surprised, Andy. Bryce is planning to ask me for a divorce. He doesn't think I know, but I do. And I'm okay with that."

"You're sure?"

"Yes. My marriage has been on life support for a long time. It's time we pulled the plug. He'll get what he wants and I'll get what I want." She wrapped her arms around his neck and tried to pull him close, but he jumped up.

"Regine, what are you doing?"

"I told you, Andy, Getting what I want. I want you."

"I told you that I'm committed to my wife."

"And I told you that Bryce is leaving me."

"So you think that frees you to hook up with me?"

"Why not? Your so-called wife is going to do the same with him. So why should we be left out in the cold?"

"Vanessa is not going anywhere."

She leaned back in her seat, crossing her arms and legs. "You're delusional, Andy. The deal you made with Vanessa will be null and void as soon as the year is up. Right about when our divorce will be final."

He leaned over, glancing around to make sure they weren't being overheard. "How do you know about that?"

"My husband isn't nearly as discreet as he thinks he is. In fact, I'm pretty sure he's with your wife right now, giving her the good news."

~ ~ ~

Andy weaved his way through the crowd, shaking hands with well-wishers along the way. He didn't see Vanessa among the guests or in the ballroom. He caught sight of Pam, who told him that Vanessa was in the ladies room but on her way back to the ballroom. Before she could stop him, he headed in that direction.

As he arrived at the corridor towards the restrooms, he heard voices. He recognized them as Bryce and Vanessa's. He stopped before they could see him.

"I can't talk about this now," she was saying.

"I know," Bryce replied. "But I just need to know if you still want to be with me."

"You know how I feel about you."

He felt a tug on his arm; it was Kendra. "We've got to go. There's trouble——big trouble."

CHAPTER THIRTY-FIVE

Hero

The car had barely stopped moving before Andy hopped out. He ran over and was restrained by a police officer that demanded to see some identification. Andy pulled out his driver's license and explained who he was. The officer lifted the Crime Scene – Do Not Cross tape, allowing him to enter the area.

An ambulance with its flashing lights was stationed nearby. Perched on the back was Adriana, blood covering her hands and clothes. An EMT was checking her over, asking her questions. When she saw Andy rushing over, she cried out, "Oh, Rev. Andy!"

"Are you alright, Adriana?"

"I'm fine," she answered, hiccupping. "The blood, it's not mine."

"Then who?"

"It belonged to the young man that was shot." A young black man spoke as he joined the two at the ambulance. "I'm Detective Smith, Chicago Police Department, Juvenile Division. I take it you're Rev. Perry?"

"That's right. What happened here?"

"Miss Vasquez was just about to fill us in." He nodded at Adriana, who began her story in halting sentences.

"I...I was finishing up our intakes for the night when a young man came in wanting a place to stay for the night. I was checking the files to see if he had previously been here, when he...he..."

Detective Smith took over. "According to Miss Vasquez, he tried to assault her."

"Oh, Adriana," Andy said. He sat next to the shaking woman, wrapping a comforting arm around her.

Detective Smith continued. "Before he could get far, Miss Vasquez cried out. One of the residents was passing by and tried to intervene. The two boys got into it and the suspect pulled out a gun and shot the other boy. Your security guy managed to subdue the suspect until the police arrived."

By now, Kendra and Ben had joined the group. Kendra was wiping her eyes as she said, "Andy, it was Keyon. He was shot. One of the officers said he died before he got to the hospital."

"Oh, dear God," Andy whispered as Adriana sobbed loudly.

Detective Smith sighed. "That's too bad. He saved Miss Vasquez tonight. Reverend, this is now a homicide investigation. We'll need to notify the boy's family. Do you have any records on him?"

Andy nodded. "In our office. I think Keyon had family in Indiana."

"We'll need those files."

"I can get them for you," Kendra said.

"Miss Vasquez, you need to be checked out at the hospital, and then come down to the station to talk to our detectives. Reverend, you'll also need to come."

Andy nodded. "Kendra, can you hang out here and get things under control?"

"Of course.

"You'll have to stay out of the offices for now. That's the crime scene."

"But our records are in there."

"I'll have one of the officers go in with you to help you get what you need." He signaled to a patrolman and instructed him to follow Kendra inside.

"It's going to be fine." Kendra hugged Adriana then went with the officer.

"Andy, let me give you a lift to the station," Ben said.

"What about Kendra?"

"She's going to have her hands full without me being underfoot. I'll come back and check on her in a while."

"What about Adriana?" Andy asked Detective Smith.

"I'll have an officer ride along with her to the hospital and they'll bring her back to the station."

~ ~ ~

On the ride to the station, Andy called Vanessa and filled her in on what happened. She offered to meet him at the station, but he was adamant that she stay away. By the time he arrived, Alexander Nichols was waiting for him. Vanessa told him what happened and he insisted on providing legal representation for both Andy and Adriana, even though they were not suspects. Alexander was joined by one of his associates, who was assigned to represent Adriana.

Andy and Alexander met with Detective Smith, while Adriana met with the homicide detectives. Andy's questioning was brief, but he decided to stay until Adriana had completed her statement.

In between fielding phone calls from his mother and Pastor Dillon, Andy tried to sort through the myriad of questions filling his head. How had this happened? How had security failed? The residents were going to need counseling. So would Adriana. It was his fault she was in this mess. What about Keyon's family? What would they say? How would they react? Would they sue? Would they blame him? If he had been there, could he have prevented this tragedy? If only I hadn't gone to the party with Vanessa.

Vanessa. That was a whole other can of worms. After hearing what happened, how would this affect the Carson family? Could the foundation be connected to this? Could they be named in a lawsuit? And what about his sham of a marriage? Would Vanessa finally admit she wanted out?

His thoughts were interrupted by Pam's arrival. "Andy," she said, "I'm so sorry about all this."

"What are you doing here?"

"Vanessa filled me in. It's all over the news. Vanessa Carson's husband is involved in a teen's murder at the shelter he operates. Front page stuff."

He winced at her use of the Carson name. "I didn't have anything to do with the actual shooting."

"That's not the point."

"Then what is?"

"The Carson family and the foundation. They are inextricably linked to all this, so it's news. The media is camped out right now waiting to pounce."

Andy shook his head. "I can't deal with all that right now."

"That's why I'm here. I've got the strategy in place to help you deal with this. As soon as Adriana is done, the police are going to release a statement. While they are doing that, we're getting out of here and heading home. Jackson is here and he has a car waiting for us."

"I've got to get back to the mission."

"I know. There are already camera crews stationed there. We'll do a quick press conference there——"

"Outside. Not inside. I don't want the privacy of our residents violated in any way."

"Understood. When we get back to the house, we'll craft a statement for you to read and we won't allow for any questions. But I have to warn you, Andy. This is not going to go away any time soon."

The door to the conference room opened and a shaken Adriana emerged with Nichols' associate. "She did just fine," the woman said. "She'll have to testify at the trial, but that's not for a while yet. We'll deal with it when the time comes."

"I'm so sorry, Rev. Andy," Adriana said, crying.

"It's not your fault. I should've been there." He saw she was still in her blood-covered clothes. He took off his overcoat and wrapped it around her. "Let's go home."

CHAPTER THIRTY-SIX

Ambush

It was dawn by the time everyone arrived at the estate. As Pam had warned, the press was waiting for the car, and as it pulled into the gated driveway, they pounced.

Jackson skillfully maneuvered the car through the throng and around to the staff entrance at the rear of the house. Carrie was already waiting for them and took Adriana into her arms. Despite the early hour, Carrie had coffee brewing. There were rolls in the oven and grits on the stove. A platter of fruit and muffins sat on the counter.

Carrie took Adriana to her room. Nichols and Pam helped themselves to some coffee and muffins. Andy headed upstairs but was stopped by an anxious Vanessa. "Are you okay?" she asked, quietly.

"Not my best night." He found it hard to look her in the face. He nodded towards the kitchen. "Thanks for sending in the reinforcements."

"It wasn't a problem. They insisted on helping. Where's Adriana?"

"Carrie took her to her room."

"She's in good hands."

"Speaking of Carrie, she cooked?"

Vanessa shrugged. "That's what she does. She prays and meditates. She says it helps her to stay focused on the Lord."

He sighed. I need to do that. "I've got to get going."

"Where?"

"To the mission. Kendra has been there all night and I need to get in and do damage control."

"But you just got here. You need to get some sleep. And I thought we could at least talk."

He held up his hands. "I can't. Not right now. There's way more at stake than whatever's going on between us." He didn't respond to her protests as he jogged up the stairs.

~ ~ ~

After showering and changing his clothes, Andy spent a few moments in prayer. Finding it hard to focus, he headed for the kitchen for a large cup of coffee and a bite to eat. Pam had already drafted a statement for him to read. He made a few additions, and then had her print it out for him. Alexander read through the final statement and gave it his blessing.

Andy opted to drive himself with Pam following. As they arrived at the mission, he could see the members of the press setting up in front of the entrance. One of Pam's associates was passing out media kits as another came over to Andy and explained what was about to happen.

Andy stood to the side as Pam introduced Andy and explained the ground rules for the press conference. Then Andy stepped up and began reading his statement. "Good morning. As you are all aware, a young resident of the Wentworth Street Mission was shot and killed last night. He interrupted an assault on a staff member by a former resident and paid for it with his life. Our security team detained the suspect until he could be apprehended by the Chicago Police Department. Our entire staff is cooperating with the Chicago Police Department during this investigation. We are grateful to them for their excellent work in the apprehension of the suspect and their sensitivity to our other residents during the investigation of this incident.

"The young man who died——to respect his privacy we will not identify him until his family is notified—— was a resident of this mission for nearly a year. He had turned his life around, excelling in school, and looking forward to reuniting with his family. Tragically, that did not happen.

"Our entire staff, board of directors, and residents are grieving in the loss of this young man. We are praying for his family. We honor him as a friend and as a hero.

"All other questions concerning this matter will be answered by the Chicago Police Department and the

Cook County State's Attorney's office. Please respect the privacy of our staff and residents during this difficult time. Thank you."

As he turned away, several of the reporters peppered him with questions. Then one person shouted, "Reverend, isn't it true that your marriage to Vanessa Carson is just a scam so she can inherit her family's fortune?"

~ ~ ~

"Sh—" Pam threw her hand over her mouth to stifle the curse.

~ ~ ~

"Oh God," Vanessa whispered, staring at the TV.

~ ~ ~

"Oh no," Ella said, "not now!"

~ ~ ~

Phoebe answered her ringing cell phone. "I'm watching now, Alexander."

~ ~ ~

Pam tried to pull Andy indoors, but he wouldn't budge. Instead, he turned back to the throng of reporters who were clamoring for a response. He held up a hand to silence them.

"Under the best of circumstances," he began, "the status of my marriage would be none of your business. As these are the worst possible circumstances to pose that question, I will only say this: the fact that you chose this moment in time to ask such a despicable question says more about you than anything that takes place between me and my wife." He turned and went inside, followed by a grinning Pam, leaving the media to ponder his words.

CHAPTER THIRTY-SEVEN

Trust

Inside Andy's temporary office, Pam spoke to the staff, reminding them to avoid speaking to the media and if confronted, to simply say, "No comment."

He barely heard a word she said. His mind kept returning to the reporter's question. He knew his response conveyed the indignance he felt at having his personal life thrown into the street, especially while he was grieving Keyon's death and anticipating the fallout.

But clearly the man knew something. Up until now, no one had even questioned his and Vanessa's sudden marriage, not since their earlier interview. Someone had talked. He thought of all the people who knew their secret. Other than Ella and Phoebe, there was Alexander, Kendra, and Pam. Alexander would never betray attorney-client privilege or the Carson family. Pam's career would be destroyed if word got out that she had undermined her most prominent client, not to mention the destruction of her friendship with Vanessa. He trusted Kendra without question.

There was only one other person to consider. Bryce Harmon. Regine's words came back to him: 'My husband isn't nearly as discreet as he thinks he is.' He must have leaked it to the reporter, hoping to force Vanessa's hand to end the marriage.

Pam was waving a hand in his face. "Andy? You still with me?"

He shook his head. "Sorry. What were you saying?"

"I was asking if you thought I should speak to the residents."

"Not yet. We've all got more important issues to deal with."

~ ~ ~

Andy spent the rest of the day counseling his residents and staff and ducking phone calls from the press. A social worker from the Department of Children and Family Services stopped by to do a surprise inspection and to offer any help to Andy with counseling or placement services if any of the residents wanted to leave. Andy was gratified to learn that no one wanted to go.

His pastor stopped by to pray with him. He also mentioned that Sis. Freeman had stopped by the church, upset over the recent turn of events. Pastor Dillon also related that a reporter asking about Andy and Vanessa's church membership had contacted him.

Under the circumstances, Pastor Dillon felt it best to call an emergency board meeting, "just to get everything out in the open."

When he finally found a few moments alone, he ducked under the yellow police tape surrounding the administrative offices. He avoided touching anything, careful not to step on any of the evidence. He stopped when he saw the reddish brown stain in the carpet. He knew instantly it was Keyon's blood——the place where the young man had fallen.

Andy knelt down, his fingers grazing the edge of the stain. He was silent, picturing in his mind what had happened. He imagined the gun going off and Keyon staggering, then falling, coming to rest, even as the blood came pouring out from his wound.

Andy closed his eyes and began to weep——for the young man whose full potential would never be realized; for his family, who lost out on a chance at reconciliation; for those residents and staff that had embraced the likeable, yet troubled, young man who was learning to find his way.

Even as he prayed for Keyon, his own troubles rose to the surface. "I don't understand any of this, Lord," he prayed. "How did everything get so out of control? Why did this have to happen to Keyon? How do I make sense of it all?"

Do you still trust Me, Andy?

"I'm trying, Lord."

I need you to trust Me, Andy. Fully and completely, with your whole heart. Even if nothing makes sense to you right now.

"But how do I do that?"

Know that I can see beyond anything you see. My thoughts, My ways, My plans are greater than anything you can imagine. You just have to trust Me.

"I'll trust You, Lord."

Good. There are going to be some dark times ahead. Just know that I love you and I will never leave your side.

"Thank You, Lord."

~ ~ ~

Jackson alerted Vanessa to Andy's arrival. She had seen the press conference, including the disastrous question thrown at him and his masterful answer. She hadn't spoken to him since their brief conversation that morning, but she wanted him to know how proud she was of him and that he had her wholehearted support.

She also knew they had to settle their personal relationship once and for all. The reporter's question had made that clear. She knew the timing of their conversation was bad, but it had to be done.

She heard him come up the stairs and enter his room. She waited ten minutes before crossing the hall. Vanessa knocked on Andy's open door then leaned against the frame. He was sitting on the edge of the bed, arms resting on his knees, hands folded up under his chin. She could see the weariness in his body. "Long day."

He nodded. "Yeah."

"Did you talk to Keyon's family?"

"Not yet. Alexander said it probably wouldn't be wise until we know if they're going to try and sue. I don't agree."

"He's just looking out for your best interests."

"Is he? He's your family attorney. And seeing as how your family has as much invested in the mission——"

"That's not fair."

He held up his hands. "I'm sorry. I'm not looking for a fight. I'm just tired." He sighed. "Did you see the press conference?"

"I did. You did a great job."

"That reporter threw me a curve ball."

"And you handled it great."

"I don't suppose that will be the end of it."

She shook her head. "Pam has already been fielding calls from reporters. As if she didn't have enough to deal with already."

"Is that my fault?"

"I didn't say it was!"

"I didn't tell the reporter about our deal! I wonder how he found out."

"Are you accusing me?"

"Not you. But I'm not so sure about your friend. Bryce."

"Bryce? Why would he do something like that?"

"He's made it no secret that he wants you. Until I came along, the only thing standing between you and him was Regine. He's already taken care of that." He noticed her stricken expression. "Yeah, I know he's filing for divorce. Now, the only obstacle that remains is me. He knows you won't leave, but if you're publicly outed, you won't have much choice but to end this."

"Bryce would never do that to me. He knows the public humiliation would be awful."

"Maybe. But then he could ride in, be the hero."

"No matter how you feel about him, he has been completely respectful of our relationship."

"We don't have a relationship, Vanessa. We have an arrangement, a sham. Isn't that what the reporter said?" He saw her wince, but he continued. "Look, I don't want to get into this with you. It's just not that important." He stood and picked up his packed duffel bag.

"Where are you going?"

"I need to leave. This is getting too messy. The last thing either of us needs is to be distracted from what we need to do."

"So, you're just leaving?"

"I need to focus on the mission right now. The residents, the staff, they're hurting. I need to help them get through this. And I need to convince the board not to shut us down."

"Can they do that?"

"I don't think so. But they can ask me to step aside. Or they can choose to walk away. Without a board, I can't keep it open, especially as a non-profit. I'm going to do everything I can to keep it open. In the meantime, I have a job to do."

"You'll be at the mission then?"

"Or at my mother's. Besides, we both need time."

"Time for what?"

"To make decisions. This was your deal. I'll abide by whatever you decide. If you want to stay married to get your inheritance, I will. If you want to end it, that's fine. As far as the financial aspect, I would only ask you to support us for one year, until I can raise funds or get the residents into proper living facilities. I also ask that you let Adriana continue her internship if she wants." He slung the duffel bag over his shoulder.

"Andy, if you leave now, people will talk."

He shrugged. "Does it really matter? I'll see you later."

CHAPTER THIRTY-EIGHT

Revelation

The headlines in the newspaper gossip column: "Could Carson Marriage Be a Fraud?" The reporter who had ambushed Andy at the press conference wrote:

The sudden marriage between heiress Vanessa Carson and the Rev. Andrew Perry came out of the blue and left many scratching their heads at such an impulsive mismatch. Now comes word that the impromptu nuptials were nothing more than a chance to claim the Carson family fortune by its sole heir.

The story went on to claim——"from a very reliable source inside the Carson inner circle"——that Vanessa and Andy schemed to meet the terms of her mother's will. Andy's part was to play the doting husband in order to ensure the fortune of his "pet project," the Wentworth Street Mission.

Vanessa slammed the paper down. "How could they print this crap?" She picked up her ringing cell phone and saw Bryce's number. "What!"

"I take it you saw the paper?"

"Of course I did! The phone has been ringing off the hook with reporters trying to get the inside scoop."

"Pam's on it?"

"Yeah. She's already drafted a statement to issue and she's planning to talk with a few of her contacts to refute the story."

"I'm so sorry about all of this, Vanessa."

She stiffened. "Bryce, tell me you weren't the inside source who gave them this."

"No! God, no, Vanessa! I know I made it clear that I wanted to be with you, but I'd never do anything to humiliate you."

"I suppose."

"You suppose? You think so little of me, of what we've meant to each other, that you'd think I'd stoop to putting your business out in the street like this?"

"You're right. I'm sorry. I had to ask."

"What made you think I'd do something like this to you?"

"Andy thought you might have done it."

"Figures. Speaking of Andy, how's he doing through all this?"

"I don't know." She blinked back the tears that began pooling in her eyes. "He's gone."

"Gone? Where? When?"

"He left a couple of days ago. He's been spending time at the mission or at his mother's. He said things were too messy."

"Nice. Some class act. Abandons you and leaves you holding the bag."

"Don't blame him. He's got his hands full dealing with Keyon's death and the fallout from that. Plus, his board is trying to shut the whole thing down. He could lose everything."

"So could you."

"You think I care about the money at a time like this? Andy's about to lose the mission! It's his life's work. He's poured his heart and soul into that place. If they shut it down, it'll destroy him. And those kids will be lost and back on the street again. Who knows what will happen to them?"

"Wow. I didn't know you cared so much about that place. You really have changed."

"Bryce."

"No, it's okay. I get it. I didn't want to believe it, but you've been telling me all along. You're in love with him, aren't you?"

She sighed. "Yes. I guess I never really stopped loving him."

"Have you told him?"

"No."

"Why not?"

"Because."

"Because?"

"Yes. Because it would never work. Andy and I were a mismatch in college and we still are. We come from two different realities. Our priorities are not the same."

"Really? It sounds to me like your priorities are exactly the same. You're not the same woman I've known, I've loved for all these years. He's the reason for that change."

"Still..."

"Don't make excuses when there are none. All I've ever wanted was to make you happy, Vanessa. But I know now that I'm not the one for you. You got a second chance at happiness. Don't blow it."

"Oh, Bryce. I'm sorry. I never meant to hurt you."

"It's okay. I mean, I'm not thrilled about losing you to another man. I'm just realizing I never fully had your heart. I guess that's my fault. How could I expect you to commit to me when I was still tied down to Regine?"

"Do you think you can work things out with her?"

"I don't know. Maybe. Our marriage was already fractured before you came along. Who knows? Miracles can happen, right?"

"I hope so."

"I'll always have a special place in my heart for you."

"Same here. And Bryce? Thank you."

"Take care of yourself, Vanessa."

~ ~ ~

Bryce hung up the phone just as his wife entered their bedroom. She sat down on the chaise lounge by the window, picked up a magazine, and flipped through it. "So," Regine began, "how is dear, sweet Vanessa?"

"How did you know I was talking to her?"

"I heard you. This empty house has an echo and your dulcet tones, my sweet, were banging off the walls. So, how is she?"

"She's under a lot of stress right now. But she's coping."

"Well, at least she has her dear husband to lean on. Oh wait, I'll bet he's feeling a bit of a strain too, what with the murder of that poor little boy and all the questions surrounding the legitimacy of his marriage."

"He'll survive."

"Oh, I suppose he will. He's a man of honor and integrity. It's too bad Vanessa doesn't know what a real man she's got in her husband."

"What are you talking about?"

She tossed the magazine aside. "What does she know about honor and integrity? What do those words mean to her? If she really understood them, then perhaps she wouldn't be in this mess right now, dragging poor Andy into it."

He looked at her curiously. "You know about Vanessa and Andy's marriage."

"You'd be surprised at what I know. Yes, I know about them. I know about their 'arrangement.' I know about you and her. And I know that you were planning to leave me."

He shook his head. "I never meant to hurt you, Regine."

"Really? Because having a long-term affair with Vanessa Carson hurts. Like having your heart ripped out and torn into pieces hurt. But then I'd imagine you know how it feels to have your heart stomped on, since she's not interested in you anymore." She stood up. "You want out? You want to be free? Fine. Be free. Not that it'll do you any good. She doesn't want you. She wants her husband. And guess what? He wants her. Everybody wants something. This time, I'm getting what I want.

"I'll grant you the divorce, but I'm getting everything I want and then some. Perhaps I'll share it with Andy. Maybe. Maybe not. Who knows?" She spun around. "I feel like a fairy godmother, granting everyone their wishes. Bryce wants a divorce? Ding! Bryce is divorced. Andy needs money to save his mission? Ding! Andy gets money. Maybe he can take in Vanessa as a resident since she'll be homeless. Ding! Ding! Ding!" She clapped her hands and laughed. "Oh yes, I can see the headlines now: Hussy Heiress to Humiliated Homeless. Won't that be perfect? Maybe then she'll understand what it's like to have her entire world turned upside down and destroyed from the inside out. Maybe then she'll know what it's like to have someone come in and destroy everything she's ever worked for and have it all blow up in her face!"

Bryce hung his head in shame. "Regine, what did you do?"

CHAPTER THIRTY-NINE

Consequences

The New Year rolled around, and with it, new tales of corruption and scandal, moving Vanessa's marital problems out of the glare of the media spotlight. Pam had woven her magic and done damage control with the press. Phoebe talked the foundation's board from asking Vanessa to step aside.

Meanwhile, Vanessa remained in seclusion at her home. Despite the departure of the media, she didn't do much to celebrate the holidays, opting to stay at home. The household staff was given their customary two-week break, leaving Vanessa alone with Phoebe in the house.

Adriana stayed behind as she continued her internship. She kept Vanessa apprised on the continuing investigation and all the happenings with the board. She also reported that Andy wasn't the same. He worked as hard as ever, but the spark he once had seemed to be missing.

Vanessa picked up the phone several times to call Andy but backed out each time. She did speak to Ella to wish her a happy new year. Andy's mother expressed her sympathy for the entire situation. She also relayed that Andy rarely spoke to her and when he was home, he stayed locked in his room. She was concerned because he hadn't been eating and was starting to lose weight.

Every night, Vanessa cried and prayed for Andy. As much as she loved him, she didn't want to see him hurt. She also knew she was the cause of his pain yet again. She just didn't know how to make his pain, and hers, go away.

~ ~ ~

Alexander Nichols stopped by on a snowy January afternoon. He handed Vanessa a manila envelope. "I brought you a copy of your mother's executed will."

"Thank you."

"I've also enclosed the annulment papers, as you requested. Once you review them and sign, I'll have my office send a copy to Andy for his signature. When that's done, we'll file the paperwork."

Vanessa nodded absently as she took the papers out and glanced at them. "Is there a time limit on signing them?"

"No. But the longer you wait, the harder it will be to get the annulment. The judge may reject it and you'll have to file for a divorce."

"Ugh. I was hoping it wouldn't come to that."

"You were probably headed in that direction anyway."

"What?"

"It's what I explained to you in the beginning. Short of a case of demonstrable fraud, an annulment after a year of marriage is very unlikely. Even on religious grounds, annulments after such a long period of time are hard to come by."

"But there's a chance?"

"Yes. It helps if there are no children involved. And if you didn't consummate the marriage... you didn't, did you?"

She blushed. "No. We never." *Though not from a lack of trying.*

"That's good. I mean, it's good for your case."

"I know what you mean."

"But you must be prepared. You're going to have to come clean about everything in front of a judge."

"Can we have the proceedings sealed?"

"Depends on the judge."

She sighed. Just when it looked like things were dying down, the thought of all of it going public turned her stomach. "What if we decided to divorce instead?"

"You could file a no-fault petition. Typically, it can be done without any specific reasons on either party's side. If Andy doesn't contest it, you could be granted the divorce in as little as sixty days and never set foot in court."

"I suppose I could always go off and get one of those quickie divorces in Reno or Mexico."

"You could, but I wouldn't suggest it."

"What about division of assets? I know I'll lose the house and most of the family fortune. What would Andy be entitled to?"

"Since you didn't sign a pre-nuptial agreement, if he decides to contest the divorce, he could claim half of what you have. We could fight that."

"Andy won't contest it."

"You're sure about that?"

"As sure as I can be. However, I did make him a promise that I would support the mission for five years."

"Did you put it in writing? Were there witnesses to the agreement?"

"No. It was just between the two of us."

"Another lawyer might argue that it was an oral contract and you are bound to it. But if he brings it up, I doubt a judge will hold you to it. If he does, we'll have to figure out what it will mean and how much it will cost you." He took her hands in his. "You don't have to make a decision about anything today. But before you do, make sure you weigh all your options. What you decide to do will forever alter the course of your life——and Andy's."

~ ~ ~

Phoebe was waiting for Alexander in the foyer. "You gave her the papers?" she asked.

"I did."

"Did you get a sense of what she's going to do?"

He shook his head. "I don't think she really knows. No matter what she decides, it's going to make her miserable. Has she said anything to you?"

"Nothing. I know she's been terribly unhappy since Andy left." She glanced upward. "I fear this is going to end badly. I've got to tell her the truth, no matter the consequences."

"Do you want me to stay, help you explain?"

She clasped his hand in his. "No, my dear friend. This is my mess. I'll have to clean it up."

CHAPTER FORTY

Help

"Miss Carson, you have a guest, Miss Kendra Rollins," Dora, the maid, announced.

"Send her in," Vanessa replied, standing.

The maid exited and returned seconds later with Kendra following her.

"Kendra. This is a surprise."

"I apologize for dropping in unannounced. I figured if I told you I was coming, you might not see me. Andy would probably kill me if he knew I was here."

"You were right, on both counts. Come in. Can I get you something to drink?"

"No, thank you."

Vanessa dismissed the maid, then led Kendra to a club chair, taking a seat opposite her. "What brings you out to the boonies in this weather?"

"I wanted to talk to you about Andy."

"Kendra."

"Wait, please. Hear me out." Vanessa didn't object, so she continued. "I feel like this is all my fault."

"Your fault?"

"Yes. I was the one that put in our application to the Carson Foundation. Andy was dead set against it because of what happened between the two of you. I pushed him into meeting you that afternoon. He had no idea he would be seeing you again. And when he told me about your proposal, I badgered him into considering it. Now, look what's happened."

"Andy is a grown man. He knew what he was getting into. This isn't your fault."

"There's something else you have to know. Andy loves you. No, scratch that. He's in love with you. He's never gotten over you."

"He told you that?"

"Yes. The night of the party."

"He never said anything to me."

"Because he was afraid of getting hurt again if you didn't feel the same way. But I know you do."

"You don't know anything."

"Yes, I do. I saw you Thanksgiving night. And again at the Christmas party. When you were dancing, I could see it all over your faces."

Vanessa hung her head. "I thought so, once. But now I'm not so sure."

"About what? How you feel or how he feels? Because I can tell you for a fact that he's still in love with you."

She glanced at the table and saw the annulment papers. "Oh. I can see how you feel."

Vanessa flipped the papers over. "My attorney brought them over. Please don't mention this to Andy."

"You don't owe me an explanation. You do what you think is best." She stood. "I'll go, but before I do, let me just say two things. First, the board meeting is tomorrow. They're either going to shut us down or kick Andy out. It would help if you could say something on Andy's behalf."

"I don't think that's a good idea under the circumstances."

Kendra frowned but continued. "Second, I know I can't tell you what to do. But I will say this. Andy didn't marry you for the money. He didn't marry you for the deal you made. If you didn't have a dime to your name and had come to him for help, he would have still married you. That's how much he loved you. Loves you." She turned to leave as Phoebe entered the room. "Ms. Carson, it's nice to see you again." She turned back. "Take care of yourself, Vanessa." She excused herself, then left.

CHAPTER FORTY-ONE

Truth

Phoebe sat down in the same chair Kendra had vacated. "I didn't expect to see Kendra here. What did she want?"

"To talk about Andy. What else?" She stood and walked towards the window. "Oh, Aunt Phoebe, I've made such a mess of things."

Phoebe smiled. "No, dear. It is I who has made a mess of things. And it's time I tried to clean it up."

Vanessa whirled around. "What are you talking about, Aunt Phoebe?"

"Come sit down." Vanessa did as instructed and the older woman continued. "You must understand that everything I've done has been in the best interests of our family, you included. It was never to hurt anyone, you understand."

"What did you do?"

"I'll get to that momentarily. First, I want you to know how much I love you. And I've grown to love Andy as well. Though I confess I did not really give him a fair shake the last time."

"What last time?"

"I now know what a truly decent and honorable young man he is. Our family would do well to have him be a part of it."

"I don't understand. What's this about? What are you saying?"

"What I'm trying to tell you is that I'm the cause of your heartache——past and present." She held up her hand to ward off her niece's questions. "All those years ago, when you were in college and dating Andy, I knew how serious the two of you had become. I also knew it wouldn't be long before he would ask you to marry him. So I sat down with your parents to discuss the situation.

"I knew he would never be able to support you in the lifestyle to which you were accustomed. I also believed that he would never want to live off our money. Your father thought that a struggling preacher would be too easily tempted to succumb to living off you. So, against your mother's objections, we made the decision that if Andy wanted to marry you, he would have to pursue his MBA and come to work for us. When Andy came to your father to ask for your hand in marriage, your father imposed those conditions, which Andy—— rightfully and wisely——refused."

Vanessa gasped. "Daddy said I would be cut off if I married him! That night at the lake, Andy sort-of proposed. When I came home and told Daddy, he was so angry. He told me I had to break up with him immediately. He made me write that note, then he put me on a plane."

"He did those things because I told him to."

Her jaw dropped. "How could you? I loved him!"

"I know. But at the time, I thought it was the best thing for all concerned."

"You had no right." Vanessa jumped up and began pacing. "I cannot believe you got my parents to go along with that."

"Your father understood what was at stake. Your mother was not pleased, but she accepted it. She never quite forgave either of us for sending you away."

"And I never would have come back. If Daddy hadn't died, I would still be anywhere else but here. I still can't believe you had the nerve."

Phoebe's calm demeanor was in sharp contrast to the shaking she felt inside. "As I said, I did what I thought was best. And anyway, I thought you'd get over him and settle down with a more acceptable young man."

"Really? How'd that work out for you?"

"There's no need for sarcasm, Vanessa."

"What would you prefer? Disgust? Dismay? How about flat out anger?"

"You have every right to be angry with me. I accept that. But I hope that you can accept that everything I

did, I've done, has been out of love and concern for your
well-being."

"You mean the Carson name, don't you?"

She nodded. "I'll admit that I was concerned about
our family's reputation, yes. It's taken a long time and a
lot of hard work to build up what we have. It only takes
one scoundrel, male or female, to destroy it."

"And you thought Andy was some kind of
scoundrel."

"I know better now."

"Great." She kept pacing, then stopped and spun
around. "Wait. You said you're responsible for my
heartache past and present. What have you done now?"

For the first time in her life, Vanessa watched her
great-aunt squirm in her seat.

"Darling, you may want to sit down."

"Aunt Phoebe."

"Please, dear." She waited until Vanessa was seated
before continuing. "I know you never really got over
Andy. And as I said, your mother never really forgave
me for my part in driving you away. After your father
died, I realized I had done a terrible disservice to both
you and your mother. I had no business dictating whom
you could fall in love and share your life with, especially
considering my lack in this area.

"When your mother learned she was ill, I realized I
would be alone and you and I would be the only
members of our family on this earth. I decided to
change that."

"What did you do?"

"When the application for the Wentworth Mission came up for their initial review, I knew what I had to do. I convinced the board to select it as one of the finalists. And when your mother died...I convinced Alexander to create the codicil to your mother's will." She hung her head down and waited for the inevitable explosion.

Vanessa stared at her aunt in shock. She grabbed the papers that the attorney had dropped off. Flipping the pages, she quickly scanned the pages searching for the codicil. Nothing. "You mean to tell me the whole marriage thing was a crock, a way to get Andy and I back together?"

Phoebe nodded. "There was nothing legal about it. As you can see, the will was executed exactly as your mother intended. You inherit the entire estate with the exception of the provisions stipulated. Alexander was reading from a carefully crafted fiction. He had no intention of altering your mother's will."

"Why were you so sure that I'd go to Andy? And what made you so sure he'd agree to it?"

"Because you were both in a desperate situation. For him to get what he needed, for you to keep what you wanted, you needed each other. The marriage was my clumsy attempt at giving the two of you a second chance at a life together."

In spite of her anger, Vanessa couldn't help but laugh. "It wasn't about the money. It was never about the money for either of us."

"Wasn't it? When your father threatened to cut you off, you broke it off with Andy. If it wasn't about the money, you would have defied your father and married him in the first place."

She has a point. I should have chosen him. I didn't.

"Unbelievable," Vanessa said, collapsing back in her chair. She let out a long, slow breath, shaking her head.

"For what it's worth, I am truly very sorry."

"For which part?" she croaked. "For breaking us up? For lying to me? For using my mother's death to further your own agenda to try and ease your guilty conscience? Or are you sorry that I've lost the only man I'll ever love forever?"

"All of it. But it's not too late, Vanessa. Go to him. Tell him the truth."

"He won't understand. Hey, I don't even understand. If I go to him with this, he'll hate us both. He'll think I've been lying to him this whole time and playing him for a fool. Plus, he's got the extra headache of trying to keep the mission open and keep his job."

"Then you have to help him. He needs you now more than ever."

"What he needs is for me to stay out of his life. Just like you need to stay out of mine." She leapt out of the chair and stormed out of the room.

"Oh, Lord," Phoebe whispered, "help."

CHAPTER FORTY-TWO

Arrangements

Andy walked into the conference room carrying only his Bible. At one end of the room sat his mother, Kendra, and Kendra's boyfriend, Ben. He nodded at them, acknowledging their presence and support.

He took the empty seat directly in front of them at the end of the conference table. Pastor Dillon was at the opposite end, with Sis. Freeman sitting on his right. She was wearing the largest hat he had ever seen, complete with feathers and bows shooting from every angle. It took everything in his power not to burst out laughing.

The other board members were seated as well, some nodding in support, others busily looking at anything but him. He now knew what Esther must have felt going before the king to protect her people. *If I perish,*

I perish. He had fasted and prayed and whatever the outcome, he had peace within his soul that the Lord was in control.

Pastor Dillon opened with prayer. "Gracious Father, we come to you today, first of all to say thank you for your love and kindness, your patience and your mercy. We ask forgiveness of our sins committed openly and in secret. We lift up the family of Keyon Parrish and ask you to continue to comfort and keep them.

"Now, oh Lord, we ask for Your wisdom as we discuss these matters here before us. We thank You for Andrew and all the work he has done for Your children. Guide us and lead us as we seek the truth and to do those things that please You. We ask all in the name of our Lord and Savior, Jesus the Christ. Amen." He looked up, then called the meeting to order.

The board secretary read the minutes from the last meeting, which were adopted into the record. She turned the meeting back over to Pastor Dillon, who was the board chairman.

"As you all know, we have called this meeting to discuss the recent events of the last few weeks and to determine if Rev. Andrew Perry is still the right person to continue overseeing the mission. Andy has decided to forgo making a statement, but he has agreed to answer any and all questions put to him by the members of the board."

Andy nodded in agreement. *Here we go.*

"First, let me start by saying that we all appreciate your efforts on behalf of the mission."

"Thank you."

"Now, let's first talk about Keyon Parrish's murder and the subsequent investigation."

Andy nodded again. "You've all seen copies of the statements made by Miss Vasquez, our security team, and myself. The police department's investigation correlates to what has been said and is concluded. The district attorney has filed charges of first-degree murder and attempted sexual assault among other things. They are working with the young man's public defender to arrange a plea deal. If he pleads guilty, he faces a minimum of twenty years. If it goes to trial and he's convicted, he'll most likely wind up sentenced to life in prison. The court will take into consideration his age and previous record and other mitigating factors before determining his sentence."

"Have you spoken to Keyon's family?" one of the members asked.

"Yes, I have. The district attorney and board counsel advised that it would be alright to do so. I returned Keyon's personal belongings to them. Keyon had been on the streets for years, into drugs and other crimes. The fact that he had come off the street and was turning his life around was a great comfort to his family. They decided not to file a lawsuit. Instead, they are creating a foundation of their own in Keyon's hometown to help provide other at-risk young people with an opportunity to succeed. We are planning to partner with them to help build this organization in Keyon's name. Part of the effort will be to create scholarships to deserving teens to go to college."

"Where will the funds come from, and how will they be administered?" another member asked.

"We have approached the Carson Foundation for a donation. Additionally we will be partnering with board members from the University of Chicago and Notre Dame University to create the guidelines. More information on that will be forthcoming."

"Speaking of the Carson Foundation, will they be continuing their financial commitment to the Wentworth Mission?" the same member asked.

"I don't have a definitive answer for you."

"How did you get the foundation's help in the first place?" another member asked.

"My assistant director, Kendra Rollins, put in the application. We were selected as one of three finalists for the grant."

"You mean your wife had something to with it, don't you?" Sis. Freeman asked, a sneer crossing her face.

Andy shifted in his seat. "It's my understanding that the decision was made by the board. Vanessa did not have the final vote in the process."

"Now we're getting to the nitty-gritty. Let's talk about your so-called wife and this sham marriage."

"Yes. Let's talk about that."

Everyone turned to see Vanessa standing in the doorway. She strode over to the table in a steel grey pinstripe pantsuit with a coordinating royal blue blouse, Prada briefcase in hand. Andy knew the look on her face. She was all about business.

"You have no business being here," Sis. Freeman charged, fuming. "This is a closed meeting."

"I have every right to be here. Andy is my husband. You're also talking about me and my family and our foundation. That makes this my business." She turned her attention to the pastor. "I'd like to be heard on these matters."

Pastor Dillon suppressed a smile. "You did bring her up, Sis. Freeman. I feel it's only fitting that she be allowed to speak on her own behalf, if there are no other objections from the board." He glanced around. Other than the feathers shaking on Sis. Freeman's hat, there were no other objections. He gestured towards a seat.

Vanessa sat down a few seats from Andy. She laid her briefcase down in front of her and folded her hands. She bowed her head slightly before speaking. "Thank you, Pastor, for your graciousness. And I'd like to thank the board for allowing me to speak at this meeting today. There has been much speculation and innuendo about my relationship with Andy, Reverend Perry." She cast a scathing glance at Sis. Freeman, whose own face hardened. "I'm here to set the record straight."

She took a quick breath and then continued. "Yes, I did ask Andy to marry me in order to fulfill the terms of my inheritance. I chose Andy because I knew him and loved him. I also knew he was a man of integrity and honor. He still is.

"As you are all well aware, the mission was days away from being shut down. I offered him a way to save it. I know how much it means to him. He was in a desperate situation and I took advantage of that for my own purposes. I am not proud of this; I'm just stating a fact."

"Hmmph," Sis. Freeman grunted.

"I know Andy's heart. I know he didn't enter into this arrangement lightly. I literally made him an offer he couldn't refuse. What I want you to know, however, is the fact that Andy is a man of his word. He honored our agreement and our vows, even when I gave him plenty of reasons not to. He could have taken advantage of me and my situation. He never did. Not once. Not ever."

"So where do you stand now?" Pastor Dillon asked.

"I've since learned that the terms of my inheritance no longer dictate our union. I've decided to release Andy from our deal and our marriage." She purposely avoided looking in Andy's direction, unwilling to face him, Ella, or Kendra. "I am taking steps to have it dissolved."

She swallowed before continuing. "As part of our arrangement, I made a deal with Andy to personally provide funding for the next five years for the mission. I will honor that agreement." She opened her briefcase and pulled out an envelope and several folders. "This is a certified check for ten million dollars for the Wentworth Street Mission." Everyone in the room gasped, except Sis. Freeman, who slammed her hand on the table.

"You think you can just come in here and buy us off after all you've done?" she spat.

Vanessa's eyes narrowed. "I'm not buying anyone off, Sis. Freeman. I'm here because I believe in Andy and the work he's doing. I believe in those kids who just want a chance to turn their lives around. This will ensure that they and any others like them will get that chance."

She opened up the folders and passed them around. "And for the record, I know there are those of you who want to see Andy removed as director, despite the fact that this was his vision from the Lord. You are entitled to your opinion and you can vote him out if you wish. But the building, the property, and all the surrounding parcels on the block have been bought and paid for. The deeds are all in Andy's name."

She couldn't wipe the smile off her face as she saw Sis. Freeman's head shaking in anger, her hat tipping lopsided on her decade old wig. While Ella and Kendra rejoiced in their seats, Vanessa closed her briefcase and stood. "You can remove Andy from the board. You can strip him as director of the mission. You can even dissolve this board and remove yourself from association from the mission. That's strictly up to you. But you cannot throw Andy or his kids out of that building, not now, not ever. Whatever it's called, Andy and those kids are going nowhere." She left the room even as they hurled questions in her direction.

~ ~ ~

She was almost out the door when she felt a tug on her arm. She turned to find Andy staring at her. "What was that?"

"You could just say thank you."

"Vanessa, you just walked inside and turned everything, including my life, upside down, and you walk out like you just ordered a pizza! At the very least, you owe me an explanation."

"Now you want to talk?"

"Alright, fine. I'm sorry I've been avoiding you. Will you explain what just happened?"

"It's like I said. I bought you the other buildings so you can expand. You can help more kids. You can build a gym, or a library, or a computer center. The foundation is going to support you as well. Between that and my donation, you can do whatever you want."

"I know you said you'd fund us, but ten million dollars? That's too much."

"It's not too much. Besides, we never agreed on an amount, so it's done." She rubbed his cheek. "I want to do this. And I certainly can afford it."

"Speaking of...what did you mean that we didn't need to get married?"

"Turns out my mother never signed the revised will. The original will was still in place." *No need to drag Phoebe's deception into this.* "So that means you're free. We're both free."

He took her hand in his. "What if that's not what I want?"

She stepped up and kissed him on the lips. "It's what's best for both of us." She took a step back and freed her hand from his. "Thank you, Andy, for everything. I'll always have you in my heart and in my prayers." She turned and exited the building.

Neither could see the tears in the other's eyes.

CHAPTER FORTY-THREE

Finished

A light snow was falling across the city, transforming the gray winter dullness into a sparkling white winter wonderland. Andy had given up trying to read after realizing he had been staring at the same sentence for the past half hour. He thought about the events of the past few hours.

After Vanessa's stunning confession and announcement, the board was in an upheaval. Most of the board members were thrilled at the mission's unexpected windfall, even if they were not exactly happy about the circumstances. Others were concerned with what Andy might do with the land and the money. Sister Freeman declared it was the work of the devil and she wanted no part of it. Pastor Dillon told her if she felt that way, she should step down from the board, which she did, along with two additional members.

Pastor Dillon tried to restore order to the meeting. Andy assured the remaining members of the board that he was just as shocked and surprised by the turn of events as anyone. Though grateful, he knew that he would need to be diligent about spending the money and would be seeking the board's counsel before making any plans.

As the meeting ended, his mother, Kendra, and Ben rushed over to congratulate him. He tried to express his delight, but he couldn't get over the fact that his greatest blessing had come with the greatest cost.

Andy went home with his mother, leaving Kendra to share the good news with the staff and residents. When they arrived home, Ella immediately began cooking. A short while later, the doorbell rang. Andy found Vanessa's chauffeur, Jackson, standing there with his belongings. "Miss Vanessa asked me to have these delivered to you," he said. "Where shall I put them?"

"In the living room, Jackson. That's fine, thanks."

The man nodded and proceeded to bring in the luggage and several boxes filled with Andy's books and personal belongings. "If you find there is anything missing, please let me know."

"I will. Thank you, Jackson."

As he turned to leave, the chauffeur spoke. "May I say something?"

"Of course."

"I just wanted to say that it was indeed a pleasure working for you. You brought a certain amount of joy to the house that had been missing for a long while."

"Thank you. How is the rest of the staff?"

"Adriana is very busy with school and her internship, as you know. Carrie is the same, though she doesn't seem to be singing quite as much these days."

"How is Phoebe?"

He shook his head. "Miss Carson is not doing so well."

"Why? Is she ill?"

"Not physically. It seems she and Miss Vanessa had an awful row and they're not speaking. It has caused Miss Carson much distress."

"What were they fighting about?"

He hesitated. "I don't know all the details. But I believe it had something to do with you and the late Mrs. Carson's will."

"Jackson."

"I'm sorry, sir. I've already said too much. I really should be going."

"Wait, Jackson. Is Vanessa okay?"

"Again, the falling out with her aunt has upset her terribly. But I suppose seeing her angry is a far site better than watching her cry all the time." Before Andy could say anything else, Jackson shook his hand and said, "I really must go. Godspeed to you, Mister...Andy."

"One last thing, please. I need a favor, Jackson."

He paused. "I don't know."

"It's not a big deal. The next time you take Vanessa
out, give me a call. I want to visit Phoebe, but I don't
want to run into Vanessa."

The older man smiled, nodded, and then walked out
the door. As he left, Ella came into the living room. "So
that's it?"

"What's it?"

"You're just going to let things go like this?"

"Yes." He went and collapsed on the couch. "It's
over."

"Just like that? I've never seen you give up so easily
on anything, except where Vanessa is concerned."

"You know as well as I do, once she makes up her
mind, there is no going back, Ma."

"Then you have to change it."

"Why? The deal's over. She got what she wanted. I
got what I wanted. End of story."

"Bull."

"Ma!"

"Don't 'Ma' me. You know as well as I do that
Vanessa is in love with you. And I know you're in love
with her. Why don't you go talk to her? Tell her how
you feel."

"Because we're done! Vanessa Carson has walked
over my heart for the last time."

"Then I must have raised a fool."

"Excuse me?"

"Baby, God didn't just bring Vanessa back into your
life to provide money. He brought her back for you.
And you're just going to sit there and turn your back

on the chance of a lifetime? If you let her go again, you may lose her forever."

"It's not just up to me, is it? I'm not going to spend another ten years of my life wondering what if. No, Ma. Vanessa walked out on us. Again. I'm done. I don't want to talk about this ever again."

CHAPTER FORTY-FOUR

Forgiveness

A few days later, Andy was sitting at his desk when Jackson called. "Miss Vanessa is going to be at the foundation for the bulk of the day. Miss Carson will be home."

"Thanks for the heads up, Jackson," Andy replied. He hung up the phone, drumming his fingers on his desk. He stood up, grabbed his keys and his jacket. He left his office, knocking on Kendra's door. He stuck his head in her doorway. "I'm heading out for a while. Personal business."

"Lunch with Vanessa?" she replied, grinning.

"It's ten in the morning."

"Brunch?"

"No. I'll be back. Mind the store." He turned and left. Kendra continued grinning.

"I got your personal business, buddy boy."

~ ~ ~

Andy thanked God for the relatively clear expressway and light mid-morning traffic. He hated being away from work, especially now that everything had changed.

He pulled into the driveway of the Carson estate, then paused before shutting off his car. What if Phoebe wouldn't see him? In light of everything that had taken place, would the Carson matriarch decide she had no reason to tolerate his presence?

He took a deep breath, whispered a prayer, and then parked. As he walked to the door, he couldn't tell if he was shaking from the cold or from being nervous. He rang the bell and waited.

Dora, the downstairs maid, opened the door and smiled. "Good morning, Rev. Andy! It's so good to see you again. We've missed you."

He returned the smile. "It's good to be missed." She ushered him in to the foyer. "How have you been, Dora?"

"I'm well. Though I have to say, it's not been the same since you've gone. Miss Vanessa is not here."

"I know. I'm here to see Phoebe."

"Of course. One moment. I'll let her know you're here." She excused herself and headed for the sitting room.

Andy looked around the foyer. The Christmas decorations had been removed, but everything else was the same as he remembered. He felt like a stranger in a place he had grown to call home.

Phoebe's arrival startled him out of his thoughts. "It's so good to see you, Andy. I've been concerned about you ever since this dreadful mess started. How are you?" she asked, giving him a gentle hug.

"I'm doing well, all things considered." He took a step back. "I should ask how you're doing. You don't look like yourself," he said, peering down at the shorter woman.

"I'm doing all right for an old lady."

"You're hardly old, Phoebe."

She grunted. "These days, I feel much older than I am." She took him by the hand and led him to the sitting room just off the foyer. "Please, take a seat. Can I get you something?"

"No thanks. I can't stay long. I just wanted to check in on you. I know I left rather abruptly, and I didn't have the chance to say a proper goodbye." He sat down across from her. "Jackson told me you've been out of sorts. He said you and Vanessa had a falling out."

She shook her head. "He shouldn't have said anything to you."

"I'm glad he did. Just because things didn't work out between Vanessa and I doesn't mean that I've stopped caring about you. You'll always be family to me."

She smiled wanly. "I appreciate the sentiment, Andy. I don't really deserve it."

He frowned. Crossing over to sit on the ottoman in front of Phoebe, he took her hand in his. "What's really going on, Phoebe? I know this business with the mission and our marriage pact leaking to the press hasn't been easy for you. I'm sorry that you had to get caught up in all that. I know how much you value your family's reputation."

She laughed bitterly. "Andy, our reputation means nothing to me anymore. It's beyond saving."

He was taken aback. This wasn't the Phoebe Carson he knew. "Then what is it? If it's about the money, you can keep it. Your family doesn't owe me anything."

"And yet, I feel as if I owe so much to you." She patted his hands. "It's not about the money. I want you to have it. You deserve it and so much more." She wiped the tears forming at the corners of her eyes.

"Phoebe, please, talk to me. Let me help."

His gentle tone and kind eyes softened her heart. "You are such a dear man. I should have seen it all along." In quiet tones, she began explaining everything to him, including her role in his and Vanessa's breakup and the fake codicil to Maris Carson's will, all in hopes of rectifying a decade-long wrong. As she finished, she said, "So you see, I don't blame you for any of this. If it hadn't been for my interference in the first place, none of this would have ever happened."

Andy sat back, his mind reeling. His mouth dropped open as he realized all she had told him. Suddenly, everything made sense. He started to chuckle.

"You're amused by all this? It's not the reaction I expected. What's so funny?"

"You are." She gasped, so he responded. "Not you, Phoebe, but what you did. You've been blaming yourself for causing our breakup. The truth is, Vanessa didn't really want to marry me in the first place."

"That's not true, Andy."

"Yes it is. If she truly wanted to marry me, if she truly loved me, she would have fought for us. She wouldn't have let anything or anyone come between us. It was as true then as it is now." He leaned over and kissed her cheek. "I appreciate you telling me the truth. And I don't harbor any ill will because of what you've told me. I love you, Phoebe. Thank you for everything." He stood. "I've got to get back to work. I'll be in touch. And, Phoebe? Forgive yourself."

CHAPTER FORTY-FIVE

"I hear you had a visitor today," Vanessa said.

Phoebe looked up from her reading to see her niece, who was standing in the doorway of the bedroom. "Yes. Andy dropped by."

"Really? Why?"

"He wanted to check up on me. To make sure I was all right." She cast her gaze downward. "I told him the truth about everything, including my part in your breakup."

Vanessa went and sat on the edge of the bed. "You shouldn't have told him."

"I wanted——I needed——to be honest with him. He deserved the truth, as did you."

"How did he take it?"

"Better than I expected. He was quite gracious. He said he forgave me."

"I'm not surprised." She stood up. "I'll let you get your rest." She started toward the door, but Phoebe called out to her.

"Vanessa, if I ask you a question, will you be completely honest with me?" At her niece's arched eyebrow, she smiled. "I know the irony of what I am asking, but please, it's important."

"Of course. Ask."

"If your father and I hadn't intervened, if we had given you our blessing, would you have married Andy?"

"It's rather a moot point, Aunt Phoebe."

"Please. I need to know."

She shrugged. "I don't know. I loved him."

"Do you still love him?"

"Yes."

"Then why won't you try to make this work?"

"It's too late, Aunt Phoebe. Too much has happened between us. It can never be the way it was. Besides, I'm leaving."

"Leaving? When? Where?"

"I'm heading back to Europe. Once I get things squared away with the board at the foundation, I'll be leaving."

"When will you be back?"

"I won't. Good night, Aunt Phoebe."

~ ~ ~

Vanessa wandered into the kitchen and was startled to see Carrie sitting at the counter. "It's late, Carrie. What are you doing up?"

"I heard you come in. I figured you'd be stopping through here."

"You know me too well."

"I've known you all your life. Whenever you had something weighing on you, you'd make your way into the kitchen to find something to snack on."

"I'm not very hungry."

"Then how about a cup of hot chocolate?"

Vanessa nodded, and Carrie went over to the refrigerator and pulled out the milk and poured it into a small pot. Setting it on the stove, she began stirring the heated milk, while pulling down two mugs from the cabinet. She added a couple of Hershey's kisses to the milk and a couple of dashes of cinnamon, stirring and humming. When it was hot enough, she poured the mixture into the mugs, adding a heap of whipped cream and a few chocolate shavings on top. She set one mug in front of Vanessa, who took a small sip.

"Mmmm...no one makes hot chocolate like you do, Carrie." She took another sip and sighed.

"I'm glad I haven't lost my touch." She sat down across from Vanessa, taking a sip of her own. "I heard what you did for Andy."

"It was the least I could do after all I've put him through."

"I wouldn't say least. It was incredibly generous. Some might say too generous, like you're trying to buy his silence."

"Is that what you think I'm doing?"

"No, but like I said, I've known you all your life. I know your heart. And I think I know his pretty well, too. If you had done nothing, he still wouldn't have betrayed you."

Vanessa nodded. "I know. He's a good man."

"That he is." They sat in silence, drinking their hot chocolate and watching the snow flurries drift outside. "You're leaving again."

"How did you know?"

Carrie shrugged. "The last time you ran because you said Phoebe and your father refused to let you marry Andy."

"That wasn't exactly true."

"I know that. You ran because you got scared, scared of what committing to a man of God would mean for you. I told you then that if you really cared for Andy the way you said you did, you should stick around and fight for him. Instead, you hopped a plane and disappeared."

"It wasn't like that."

"Wasn't it? I understand. You were young, unsure of yourself. You thought you needed the material trappings of this world and you were afraid that you wouldn't be able to live without them."

"I'm still that way, I guess. After all, I was so afraid of losing everything, I blackmailed my former fiancée into marrying me."

"He wouldn't have done it if he didn't want to."

"He needed my money."

"Maybe. But I watched the two of you. I know he loves you. I believe you love him. Am I right?"

"Yes."

"Then why aren't you sticking around to fight for him? You know now you still will inherit everything despite what Phoebe tried to do. So why won't you stay?"

"Because being a part of my world is not what Andy wants."

"Have you asked him what he wants?"

"I don't have to. I know him as well as you know me. It's for the best, Carrie." She pushed her mug away. "Thank you for the hot chocolate. Good night. Sleep well."

CHAPTER FORTY-SIX

Andy spent the next two weeks enmeshed in his work, hiring a business manager, and meeting with lawyers, architects, and designers to discuss the future of the property on the block. With Keyon's murder case closed, the police released the crime scene. Andy and Kendra had the offices cleaned and refurbished.

As he stared out of his office window, he wondered what the future would hold in store for him. His thoughts were interrupted by a knock on his door. "You have a visitor," Kendra said.

Andy stood but was disturbed when Bryce Harmon walked through the door. He stared at Kendra, who took the hint and exited, closing the door behind her. "You're the last person I expected to see here."

"So this is the famous Wentworth Street Mission I've heard so much about."

Andy sat back down. "What are you doing here, Bryce? Did you come to gloat?"

"I heard you came into some money and I thought you could use my services." He chuckled at the absurdity of his own words as he sat down. "No, really, I just came to see for myself what it was that managed to upend so many lives." He glanced around the room. "Vanessa has good taste."

"Why are you here?"

The smile left Bryce's face. "I came here to speak to you in person. I want to apologize."

That caught Andy off guard. "Apologize? For what?"

"For getting in the way of you and Vanessa."

"There's nothing between us."

"That's not what she said."

"What are you talking about?"

Bryce grew incredulous. "You really don't know? She's in love with you. She always has been."

"She told you that?"

"Yes, she did. I had a feeling for months now, but she didn't come right out and say it until I finally asked her."

Andy turned away. "Even if that were true, it's too late for us." He picked up a stack of paper and waved it in the air. "Divorce papers. Vanessa's lawyer sent them over." He tossed them back on the desk. "I guess you can finally get what you wanted."

"I wish."

"Excuse me?"

"The only thing I'm getting out of all of this is a divorce from Regine."

Andy frowned. "I know. I'm sorry about that. The night of the party, she told me she thought you were going to file."

"Yeah? Did she also tell you that she was the one who told the reporter about your marriage deal?" Seeing Andy's shocked expression, he continued. "Yeah. I found out that same day you were ambushed. She admitted it. No shame whatsoever. She wanted to pay Vanessa back for our affair. It seems she also wanted to give you a little smack down for rejecting her."

Andy shook his head. "I just assumed it was you."

"Wanna know the kicker? I checked her cell phone records. She'd been having an affair with this guy for weeks, promising him the scoop of a lifetime. She waited until the worst possible moment to throw it in your faces."

"To think I once considered her a friend."

"And to think I once considered spending the rest of my life with her. Yeah, we're both suckers. I know I'm not innocent in all this, but I would never have resorted to public humiliation." He stood. "I didn't come here to talk about all this. I really just came to tell you if you and Vanessa want to be together, you'll get no interference from me or my soon-to-be-ex."

"You and Vanessa are done?"

"Haven't you been listening to a word I've said? We've been done! I just didn't want to accept it. It wasn't until the night of the party that she told me once and for all that it was over between us. She told me she didn't love me; she was in love with you. Even though I held out a little hope, the truth is, I knew back on the island that we were done. It just took my heart a little longer to accept it."

"I won't say I'm sorry things didn't work out for you," Andy said. "But it's over for me as well."

"What's wrong with you? How many chances do you think we get in this life to experience love? Look at me. I'm a two-time loser. But you? You're a bigger fool than I thought." He turned and walked out the door.

In seconds, he was back. "Vanessa is on a flight tonight to London. She's not coming back." He left again.

Andy sat, tapping his fingers on his desk. Bryce's words echoed in his ears. *How many chances do you think we get in this life to experience love? You're a bigger fool than I thought.* His mother's words also permeated his thoughts: *I must have raised a fool.*

Just as quickly, the words of both Psalms and Isaiah rose up in his spirit. *O Lord, how great are Your works! Your thoughts are very deep. A senseless man does not know nor does a fool understand this.*

In a moment of clarity, Andy knew what he had to do. He picked up the phone and dialed. "Jackson? It's Andy. I need a huge favor."

CHAPTER FORTY-SEVEN

Redux

The wet snow began coming down in earnest as the sun began to set. Vanessa's pilot checked the weather radar and informed her that it would be best to wait a couple of hours and ride out the worst of the storm at the airport.

Two hours later, the storm showed no sign of letting up. She spoke with the pilot and made arrangements to reschedule her flight for the next day, then arranged for a suite at a hotel near the airport. She was about to arrange for a limo to pick her up, when the terminal manager informed her that her car had arrived. Confused, Vanessa walked over to the terminal entrance as the car pulled forward. "Jackson?" she called out. "I didn't call for you. What are you doing here?"

The door opened, and Andy got out, grinning. "I thought you could use a ride home."

"Andy! How? Why are you here?"

"I told you. I thought you could use a ride home."

"I'm on my way to Europe."

"I know that. But there's a storm moving in. I figured you weren't going anywhere, at least not tonight."

"I'm leaving first thing in the morning." She turned and went inside the terminal.

He was right behind here. "Maybe. Maybe not. Something tells me you're not going anywhere."

She turned so abruptly, he bumped into her. He grabbed her shoulders to steady himself. She scowled at him and he released her. "You can't stop me from leaving."

"I can't, but God can. In fact, he already did."

"Really."

"Yes, really."

She crossed her arms and shifted her weight on one leg. "How did you know I was here? And that I was leaving?"

"A little birdie told me. A flock of birdies."

"Um-hmm. Make yourself useful and ask Jackson to come in to get my things."

"Nope."

"Excuse me?"

"I'm not asking Jackson to do anything until you and I talk."

"There's nothing to talk about. We've said everything that needs to be said."

"No, you said everything. You never gave me the chance to say anything."

"We're not doing this. Especially not here."

She turned away from him. "Oh yes, we are." He took her by the arm and spun her around so she was facing him. He eased the pressure, but didn't release her this time. "Jackson is staying in the car and I'm not letting you leave until you hear me out."

The lounge manager noticed the couple and began moving in their direction. "Is everything all right, Miss Carson?"

She held up a hand. "It's fine. My friend has an important message."

The manager looked back and forth between the two of them, nodded and backed off. He still wore a wary expression. Andy thought it best to take a step back before the manager felt the need to call security.

"I'm sorry," Andy said. "I don't want to cause a scene."

She sighed. "You said you had something to say. Fine. Speak."

Now that he had her attention, he didn't know how to start. *Help, Lord!*

Talk to her like you're talking to Me.

"I'm waiting," Vanessa said.

"I know. Well, uh.... First, I just want to say thank you. For everything. For bailing out the mission. For convincing the foundation to stick with us. For standing up for me with the board. You changed my life. You changed a lot of lives."

"You're welcome. Is that all?"

"No! I also want to tell you I love you."

"I love you, too."

"No, you don't understand. I don't just love you. I'm in love with you. I am truly, madly, deeply, head over heels, heart on my sleeve in love with you." When she didn't respond, he continued. "I know you don't believe me. I certainly haven't given you reason to believe me. But it's true.

"The night of the party, I told you I believed God brought us together again for a reason. I still believe that. What I didn't get to tell you that night was that I love you. I want to spend the rest of my life with you. You are the one that God designed for me. Even after you left, even though my heart was broken, I still loved you. That day in the restaurant when you made your ridiculous proposition, I knew then that I loved you. When you asked me to marry you, I wanted to shout yes to the world, but my pride got in the way. I love you, Vanessa Carson, and I will go on loving you until the day I die."

He reached into his coat pocket and pulled out a small box. "I know you love me, Vanessa. In spite of all we've been through, all we've said and done to each other, I know you love me. Ten years ago, I told you how I felt and that I wanted to marry you." He pulled her close. Leaning in, he whispered, "I know the pressure your family put you under. I know why you ran. I'm asking you not to run again." He put the box in her hand and stepped back.

Despite her best efforts, Vanessa couldn't stop her hands from trembling. She opened the box and gasped.

It was the exact same ring Andy showed her while they were walking on the lakefront. "I can't believe you still have this," she whispered.

"It's your ring. It was always meant for you." He dropped to one knee. "I love you, Vanessa Carson, heart and soul. Will you marry me – again? This time, for real?"

CHAPTER FORTY-EIGHT

Beloved

"You don't have to do this," Kendra said. "At the very least, we could have done this at your house."

"Nonsense," Vanessa replied. She adjusted the veil around her shoulders. "This was my idea. It's the perfect place to do this." She smiled even as Kendra shook her head.

"At least we know the food will be good. Carrie has been working those kids all day."

There was a knock on the door, then Phoebe entered, smiling. "Oh, my dear. You look lovely. Your parents are surely smiling down on you today."

Vanessa rushed over and gave her aunt a hug and a kiss on the cheek. "Thank you, Aunt Phoebe. I think so too." She went back over to stand in front of the full-length mirror, smoothing down the wrinkles in her gown. She had chosen a simple charmeuse v-neck halter dress with a dropped waist and beading just above the hip line. The dress was elegant, but the material flowed gently, allowing her to move freely down the aisle.

Pam stuck her head in the doorway. "It's time. Last chance to duck and run. I've got Jackson on standby," she said, laughing.

"Not a chance," Vanessa replied. "Let's do this." Vanessa took the bouquet of purple orchids and white roses from Kendra, who followed Pam out the door. Vanessa wrapped her arm around Phoebe's and the two of them walked down the hall towards the common room.

"Thank you for letting me be a part of this," Phoebe whispered.

"I wouldn't have it any other way."

The doorway of the room was draped in purple and silver draperies. Clear Christmas lights twinkled around the room, which had been transformed into an intimate chapel. The chairs were covered in white covers tied by purple bows. All of the Wentworth Street Mission residents were dressed in their best clothes and were joined by members of Andy and Vanessa's church.

As Vanessa and Phoebe began walking down the aisle, the room erupted into a series of cheers and whistles from the teens and young adults. Vanessa laughed out loud. She had grown to love these kids as much as Andy and they were thrilled to be a part of their wedding. As she reached the end of the aisle, she reached over and hugged a beaming Ella.

Andy stood at the altar with Ben at his side. He was beaming, but he only had eyes on Vanessa. He stepped up and hugged Phoebe, who kissed her niece and placed her hand in his. The two of them stared at each other for a long moment, only turning when they heard Pastor Dillon's voice. "It's been a long time coming, but I am so glad to be here to finally say: Dearly beloved."

ACKNOWLEDGEMENTS

First and foremost, I give thanks to God, for it's through Him that I am and I do. I am eternally grateful for the gift of salvation through Jesus Christ. I thank Him for giving me the talent to write. I pray that I will always use it to glorify Christ and His kingdom.

To my husband, Marvin: You are my first, my last, and my everything. Thank you for your love and affection. Thank you for being such an amazing husband and father. Thank you for showing that a real man prays, cooks and cleans! (That's what true sexy is!) Thank you for giving me the time and space to do this writing thing and for your unwavering support. I love you more than words can say.

To my mini-me, Matthew: I know you don't always get it when Mommy is "working," but I hope what I do inspires your own creativity. Thanks for being my cheerleader! I love you, Boo-Boo.

To Joey and Rasheeda: May you have many years of love and happiness!

To my editor, Michelle Chester of EBM Professional Services: You not only rock as an editor, but you push

331

me like no one else. I am so glad we are more than friends; we are sisters! I am so proud of you for embarking on the greatest journey of your life. Before long, you'll have enough material to write your book! Special thanks to my cover designer, Vonda Howard. Your design literally took my breath away. You rock!

To my 369 Divas, Daphine Glenn Robinson ("Big Sis") and Cherlisa Starks-Richardson ("Baby Sister"): I couldn't have done this without you. Thank you for your prayers, for your comments and critiques, for kicking my tail (aka encouragement), for making me laugh and letting me vent. But most of all, thanks for walking this journey with me. Love you to life, besties!

To my Godmother, Willie Mae Hackney: There aren't enough words to tell you how much you mean to me and how you've blessed and changed my life. God knew exactly what he was doing when Mama brought you into my life. I love you, Mama Dear!

There are so many others who have poured into and supported me over the years. I want to give a shout out to my siblings, Victor and Talese, Kenneth and Avis; my aunts Ruby, Betty, Deloris, Laura and Emma; my uncles Gene, Willie and Sam (miss you Uncle David and Uncle Marvin); my thousand and one cousins (including my literary cohort, Kendra); my nieces and nephews (Auntie Donna loves you!); my Providence and

Salem Baptist Church families; my literary she-ros: ReShonda Tate Billingsley, Victoria Christopher Murray, Bettye Griffin, Angela Benson and Ella Curry; BWRC director Tia Ross and the coolest literary chick on the planet, Mondella Jones; all the many, many writers and authors who I've had the pleasure to meet along the way – I truly thank you all.

To Ernest and Carryola Dickson: I love you and miss you Ma & Daddy. I'll see you in Glory one day.

To those of you who have chosen to purchase and read my novel, I hope you find inspiration, laughter, love and romance! Thank you from the bottom of my heart.

ABOUT THE AUTHOR

Donna Deloney has been an avid reader since age three and has been writing most of her life. She came in second place in the Black Expressions Book Club fiction writing contest. She has been a featured presenter at the Black Writers Reunion & Conference and the Faith & Fiction Retreat. *A Decent Proposal* is her second novel. Her first novel, *Journey to Jordan*, will be rereleased in January 2014.

In addition to being a wife, mother and grandmother, Donna enjoys singing, participating in children's creative ministries at her church and freelance editing. She resides in Chicago with her family.

Made in the USA
Monee, IL
07 February 2025

11819024R00193